THE INCREDIBLE DADVENTURE

Books by Dave Lowe

The Incredible Dadventure
A Mumbelievable Challenge
The Spectacular Holly-Day

The Stinky and Jinks series:
My Hamster Is a Genius
My Hamster Is an Astronaut
My Hamster Is a Spy
My Hamster's Got Talent
My Hamster Is a Pirate
My Hamster Is a Detective

Squirrel Boy Vs The Bogeyman
Squirrel Boy Vs The Squirrel Hunter

THE INCREDIBLE DADVENTURE

BY DAVE LOWE

Illustrated by The Boy Fitz Hammond

Piccadilly
PRESS

First published in Great Britain in 2017 by
PICCADILLY PRESS
80–81 Wimpole St, London W1G 9RE
www.piccadillypress.co.uk

Text copyright © Dave Lowe, 2017
Illustrations copyright © The Boy Fitz Hammond, 2017

A CIP catalogue record for this book is available from the British Library.

ISBN: 978-1-8481-2586-5
also available as an ebook

1

Printed and bound by Clays Ltd, St Ives Plc

Piccadilly Press is an imprint of Bonnier Zaffre Ltd,
a Bonnier Publishing company
www.bonnierpublishing.com

For my dad, Graeme Lowe, the king of the treasure hunts

1 The Birthday Card

I'm ten tomorrow. Ten, at last. Double figures.

Last month, Emily Fellows turned ten and got a birthday card that was bigger than her head (and Emily Fellows has a really, really big head).

A boy in my class got a superhero birthday card from his mum and dad, and brought it into school to show everyone. Every time he opened it, Batman and Superman popped up and said, 'Have a Super Day!'.

My birthday cards are different. Very different.

My dad makes them himself.

There is always a rhyme inside, but of course normal birthday cards have rhymes too, even if they're not usually as funny as my dad's. No, the really unusual bit is the front of the card. It's always divided into six squares. In the first square is my name and age. In the others are really bad stick drawings of Notable Events from my last twelve months.

I love those cards. Whenever I go to sleep on the night before my birthday, I'm thinking about all the presents that I might get of course – I'm not a complete weirdo – but I'm also wondering just what will be on this year's card.

Mum secretly likes Dad's cards too, though she sometimes pretends that she can't understand what his drawings are supposed to be, or complains that he chooses the silliest events from each year instead of the most important ones.

For example, this is last year's card:

Here is my mum getting stuck on the slide in the park. It was hilarious.

This is me getting third place in the school Under-9s breaststroke. (There were only four entrants, and Hayley Sanders forgot how to do it halfway and had to be rescued.)

Here's the time Dad attempted the Mega Burger Challenge at Beefy's Steakhouse. (That was also the night that Mum broke the World Record for Most Tuts in One Hour.)

Here is our dog, Oates, at his Disobedience Class.

And here's my new baby brother, Ernest. This is a picture of his first-ever smile, which came after about two months of continuous screaming.

So, while other parents might give their kids super-fancy birthday cards, my dad's ones are daft, unique and brilliant. Three words which also describe my dad.

Even his job is unusual. I tell people that he's an explorer, though my mum says that he's actually a travel writer. But Dad doesn't go to posh hotels in Italy and write about how comfy the pillows are. He goes on expeditions to jungles and deserts and dangerous places like that, and then writes funny articles about his adventures for newspapers and magazines.

That's where Dad is right now: on one of his expeditions. He's writing a book called *Have an Ice Day*, about a journey through some really cold countries. He'll be spending a night in an igloo in Finland, travelling by dog sled in Sweden and herding reindeer in Greenland. He's already been away for three weeks, and he'll be gone for another two at least.

Dad being away was one of the reasons I was feeling sad on the way back from school. Mum and I were walking home with Ernest (crying in his pushchair) and Oates (tugging on his lead, and the only one of us who wasn't in a bad mood. Oates is much too excitable to ever be grumpy).

We'd stopped off at the park on the way home, as usual, so Oates could have a run around. He has a very simple life, even for a dog. His hobbies are chasing things (sticks, balls, other animals, his own tail, et cetera), sniffing things (mostly trees and other dogs' bottoms) and getting really dirty.

It was this last hobby of his, in fact, that was the reason for my mum's bad mood. He'd managed to find the only patch of mud in the entire park and then, before

I could stop him, he'd rolled happily around in it like he was a small, hairy hippopotamus.

So, as we turned the corner into our street, Oates was filthy, Mum was furious, and Ernest, in his pushchair, was still wailing. This was not unusual. He was probably hungry, or tired, or bored. Maybe all three. With Ernest, it is almost impossible to tell.

I'd had another bad day at school.

Ms Devenport had been talking about jobs and then she'd gone around the class asking everyone what they would like to be when they grow up. Emily Fellows and the Harmer twins all wanted to be ballet dancers, of course, and Jade Skinner said that she was going to be a vet (though I really wouldn't want to be a gerbil that had its life in Jade Skinner's hands). Most of the boys wanted to be either footballers or spies, or both – you know, secret agents who play in midfield for Real Madrid at the weekend.

When it was my turn, I said 'explorer'. There was a lot of giggling. Ms Devenport had to shush the class, and Emily Fellows whispered something mean about me needing a map just to find my way to the toilet. I turned bright red, as usual, and stayed quiet for the rest of the day.

As we walked home, I was still feeling upset. And I was really, really, really missing my dad.

That's the only bad thing about his job – he's away so often that he misses loads of important things. This time, he wouldn't be here to see my (probably

8

humiliating) performance in the school talent show next week, and he was also going to miss my birthday. To make matters worse, he didn't even leave a card behind. I'd asked Mum a few days ago, and she said that he'd left two presents for me, but no card. He must have been so busy planning for his trip – making arrangements and packing extra-warm clothes – that he completely forgot about it.

With no Dad and without even a special birthday card to cheer me up, tomorrow just wouldn't be the same.

We walked up our path and Mum opened the front door, tried to calm Ernest and attempted to block Oates from getting in. I helped Mum with holding Oates back until she said, 'There's something special for you in the kitchen, Holly.' I gasped with excitement, let go of the muddy dog and dashed inside. Oates followed me in.

And there, on the kitchen table, was a medium-sized, flat envelope, addressed to me in my dad's unmistakable handwriting. It had four Norwegian stamps. I snatched it up, ripped it open and whooped with delight. Inside was a letter, and another, smaller envelope: a birthday card!

On the front of that envelope was 'NOT TO BE OPENED UNTIL YOUR BIRTHDAY'.

So I read the letter instead.

Dear Holly,

How are you? I'm fine, but a bit cold – brrrr! – and I'm really missing you and Mum and Ernest and sometimes even Oates, though I don't really miss his drool.

This year's birthday card is a bit different, as you'll see. About a week before I set off on this expedition, you said to me how unfair it was that I get to go on amazing adventures around the world and you have to stay home.

Well, travelling is my actual job, and school is very important for you, to fill that enormous brain of yours with new stuff, but I do see what you mean. So I've made you a Dadventure! I know that you're at home, but there are still lots of incredible new experiences and exciting adventures to be had.

The first task is in your birthday card. No peeking!

There are ten tasks to be completed in ten days.

Some of them are very silly. Some are serious. Some are easy-peasy. Some are not so easy-peasy. And some – just a few – are completely death-defying (but don't tell Mum about the death-defying bit).

So good luck, have fun and be brave.

Love you times a million,

Dad x

P.S. What do you call an Eskimo house without a toilet?
An ig.

2 The Dadventure Begins

Getting to sleep the night before my birthday is never easy. But this time was even worse than usual – on top of all the birthday things to look forward to, I had the start of the Dadventure too. I was wriggly with excitement.

I slipped the envelope under my pillow, lay down and tried to sleep, but it was impossible. I tried counting sheep, which sometimes works, but not this time: the imaginary sheep turned out to be having adventures of their own – being shot out of cannons like high-speed clouds, or bungee-jumping off a cliff. And thinking about bungee-jumping sheep doesn't really make you drowsy.

It was absolutely ages before I fell asleep and so when I woke up in the morning I was really groggy. It was a few seconds before I even realised it was my birthday, and a few more seconds before I remembered Dad's card.

I groped under my pillow for it, pulled it out and tore open the envelope.

Instead of the usual stick drawings on the front of the card, there was a map: a funny treasure map like you might find in an old book.

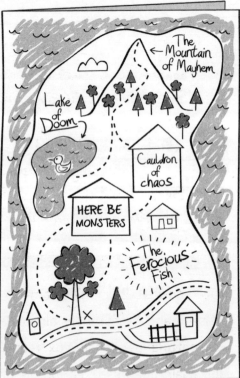

On the inside was 'Happy Birthday, Holly!' And below that was a poem: the first task.

It wasn't quite the hair-raising, spine-chilling, daredevil adventure that I'd been hoping for. But it did at least make me laugh.

Task 1:
I thought we'd start with something easy.
Something lovely, something squeezy.
Give Ernest a hug, give Mum a smooch
(But you don't need to worry about
kissing that pooch).
See – I told you it wasn't really bad.
Miss you times a billion – your very proud Dad.

I raced downstairs in my pyjamas.

Mum and Ernest were already in the kitchen. Mum was getting my lunch box ready. Ernest was in his high chair, but wasn't *eating* his breakfast so much as painting his face with it. Oates normally hangs around when anyone is eating, so he can snaffle up the scraps, but right now he was hiding under the table avoiding the splashes of orange baby slop. If Oates didn't fancy eating something, then you knew it had to be very disgusting indeed. Ernest's breakfast was the colour of earwax, and only slightly more appetising.

Avoiding a glob of baby food on the floor, I stepped over to Ernest, hugged him (he looked a bit startled) and when I located a breakfast-free spot on the top of his head, I gave him a little kiss there.

'Happy Birthday, Chicken!' Mum said when she noticed me. I walked over to her and, on tiptoes, gave her a hug and a peck on the cheek.

'Ah,' she said. 'Task number one, I see.'

'Did Dad tell you what all the tasks are?' I asked, unable to hide my disappointment, but she shook her head.

'Just the first one,' she said. 'Have some toast, and I'll bring your presents over. Dad said that the second task is inside one of his presents.'

I sat down, but I was much too excited to eat.

I didn't mind the first task being easy – not at all – but I wanted the next one to be a real adventure.

I wanted to laugh in the face of danger. To tickle the toes of terror. To pluck the nostril hair of peril . . .

Mum brought over the presents: from my grandparents and uncles and aunties, plus one from Mum, one from Ernest, and two presents from Dad – one was an untidy bundle and the other was a rectangular box. You could tell the ones Dad had wrapped. Mum's present was wrapped in shiny paper and held together by three tiny squares of sticky tape. Dad's looked like he'd had a wrestling match with an entire roll of wrapping paper, and lost.

But of course it was Dad's presents that I opened first.

I tore the paper off the bundle – a pair of walking boots! Dark green with deep treads and silver reflective strips – they looked like something a real adventurer would wear.

Then I excitedly unwrapped his other present and this time revealed . . . a box. The box that the shoes had come in! I wondered if this was one of my dad's jokes – an empty box – but then I saw that he'd crossed out the name of the brand of shoes and scribbled 'Holly's

Adventure Kit' on it instead. I opened it up and peered inside.

There was a small pair of binoculars. A whistle. A water bottle. A penknife. A mini pad of paper and a pencil. A box of Band-Aids. A bag of sweets. A key. And an envelope with 'Task 2' written on the front. I ripped it open.

Task 2:
To show that you're a daredevil (like me),
Climb to the top of Lofty the tree.
(Come on! Be brave! Don't be a wimp!
Just think like a monkey. Or a chimp!)

I stared out of the window into the garden. There was the tree that Dad meant: the one he'd named 'Lofty'. It had a thick trunk and wide branches. And it was as tall as the house.

I gulped. I felt sick.

What on Earth was Dad thinking? He knows that I'm completely terrified of heights! It started on the school trip to Mount Never-rest, the indoor rock-climbing centre. I'd really been looking forward to it. Other kids are good at art or music, or they're super-smart. Some kids are good at everything. Not me. But rock climbing – it seemed kind of adventurous, kind of daring, like it might be my sort of thing.

When it was my turn to climb, I reached halfway without too much trouble, but then I looked down. Big mistake. I completely froze. It's like my body shut down: my chest tightened, my breathing became fast and shallow and my hands just wouldn't move. I could hear the instructor below – Jim – telling me to relax, but it just made me grip the wall even more tightly. I could also hear the unmistakable giggles of Emily Fellows and her gang.

They teased me for weeks afterwards in class. 'Her dad's climbed mountains,' said Emily Fellows to Jade Skinner, in a voice just loud enough for me to hear, 'but Holly Chambers can't get halfway up a wall without completely freaking out.'

So – heights are definitely not my thing.

I passed the note to Mum, who read the task and shook her head.

'Your father has finally lost his mind!' she said. Oates pricked up his ears and looked at Mum. 'I won't allow it,' she said. 'Definitely not.'

The funny thing was, I was actually disappointed to hear Mum say that. I'd been craving a challenge, and here it was. It was pants-wettingly terrifying, yes. But although I felt sick with nerves, I wanted to do it. I couldn't give up, not on Day One! Not if I wanted to call myself a great adventurer.

'I've got to do it, Mum.'

'Last month you were too scared to climb the step ladder.'

It was true. 'But . . .'

'Open your other presents,' she said with a gentle smile. 'And leave Dad to me.'

My present from Ernest was a magic wand: a trick one, with instructions. It was really nice, but right now it made me think of the talent show – which wasn't a nice thought at all.

From my nans and granddads I got penguin stuff. Again. I sighed. When I was five, they'd all taken me to the zoo and I'd been completely obsessed with the penguins there. My grandparents had never forgotten this and every Christmas or birthday from then on I'd been given something penguin-y. So far, I have five stuffed toy penguins, a penguin egg cup, a penguin piggy bank, the *Happy Feet* DVD, a penguin onesie, two penguin key rings, a penguin hat, a penguin game called *Hey, That's My Fish!*, a picture book called *Penguins in Peril*, a chapter book called *Penguin Pandemonium*, a penguin jigsaw, penguin socks, Penguinopoly (like Monopoly but with penguins) and a mechanical penguin that poos out cola-flavoured sweets. Basically, what I'm saying is I have a lot of penguin stuff. And I don't have the heart to tell my grandparents that I'm not so keen on penguins any more.

Today – surprise, surprise – I got a pair of penguin slippers. And you'll never guess what flightless, black-and-white Antarctic bird was on my new T-shirt.

My present from Mum was also something to wear, but something even more strange – a bow tie.

I frowned. I didn't want to seem ungrateful, but some people at school make fun of me already – Emily Fellows and Jade Skinner and the Harmer twins. Laughing at me seems to be one of their hobbies. Mostly it's because I don't really fit in. I'm a girl who doesn't like pink or dancing or the latest clothes. I get called a tomboy, but I don't really fit in with the boys either.

I'm often the odd one out. This never used to bother me much, but the teasing from Emily and her gang has been really getting to me recently. And if any one of them spotted me wearing a bow tie, it would be the icing on the cake.

'I thought you could wear it on stage,' said Mum. She smiled, picked it up, pressed a button on the back, and the bow tie lit up and spun around. 'I thought, if things are going badly – which they definitely won't, by the way – but if they are, you can just press the button and create a distraction, make everyone smile.'

I tried not to look annoyed. People would be smiling, all right. Laughing, even. And not in a good way.

If there's one thing that scares me more than heights, it's making a complete idiot of myself in front of all the kids in my school. In front of Emily Fellows and her friends: all waiting for me to fail. In front of teachers and parents.

It was Dad who'd talked me into trying out for the talent show – somehow he'd managed to persuade me that facing my fears head-on was a brilliant way of overcoming them. And, unbelievably, I'd passed the audition. I'd done a simple card trick – pretty clumsily, I thought – but Mrs Stanley, the drama teacher, had yelled enthusiastically, 'You're in!'

She must have been desperate though, because only twelve kids in the whole school had auditioned and one of those was Harrison Duffy, whose entire act was him making music with his armpit.

Dad says that being an individual is important, and that he's very proud of me, but *he* doesn't have to go to school any more. I don't want to be different. I don't like to be noticed. And yet, in ten days' time, I'd be on stage, alone, with absolutely everyone staring at me. I was completely dreading it. But maybe if I could face my fear of heights, it would make me feel a tiny bit braver about the school show.

On the way to school I pestered my mum to let me climb Lofty, but she wasn't budging – until I used a tactic that I could only use once a year.

'Please, Mum,' I said, 'it *is* my birthday.' Then I stared at her with my best puppy eyes.

She sighed one of the longest sighs in world history. In fact, it started out as a sigh but ended as more of a

groan. And then she said, 'If you're going to do it, Holly, the key word needs to be "safety".'

And that's how, after school, I came to be in the garden at the foot of Lofty, wearing the knee pads, elbow pads and helmet from my rollerblading phase. I felt pretty stupid having to wear so much protective equipment, but considering how safety-mad Mum is

I suppose I should have been grateful that she hadn't actually rolled me up in bubble wrap.

She was standing in the garden, hands on hips, looking even more nervous than I was.

'Be careful!' she said, as I pulled myself up onto the first low branch. I know she was only trying to help, but she was fully stressing me out. 'If you fall and break something, you'll have to miss the talent show. It's pretty hard to pull a rabbit out of a hat with two broken arms.'

The thought of missing the talent show actually made tumbling out of the tree pretty tempting.

Ernest was crawling around on the grass. Oates was barking encouragement. At least I think he was. He might have spotted a cat.

I tilted my head back and looked up. The top of the tree was really, really far away. I could make out a small metal box clumsily sticky-taped to a high branch. I imagined my dad climbing the tree and hiding the box while I was at school one day, before he went on his expedition.

'We can get the ladder,' Mum said, probably sensing how incredibly nervous I was. 'Dad's note didn't say anything about not using ladders.'

I shook my head. 'No, Mum,' I said, firmly. 'That would be cheating. I've got to do it myself.'

Then I took a deep breath, and reached up to the next branch.

3 Lofty

When I was halfway up, Mum said, 'Great job, Holly! Now, whatever you do, don't look down!'

Which, of course, made me look down straight away.

The ground was a long, long way away. I gasped. Wobbled. Felt dizzy.

But managed to cling on.

And then it was like the rock-climbing disaster all over again: I was so terrified that I couldn't move. My cheek was tight to the rough bark, and I was gripping the trunk – hugging Lofty like I'd hugged Dad before he left. Dad calls those hugs 'bone-crunchers'. I was bone-crunching the tree trunk!

'You all right, Sausage?' said Mum from the ground.

'Just resting!'

'It doesn't look very restful,' she said.

'I'm good!'

But I wasn't good at all.
My body just . . . wouldn't . . . move.
It felt like one tiny movement of an
arm or leg might send me toppling
backwards and hurtling towards
the ground, so I clung to the tree as
if my life depended on it. Because
it probably did.

The rock-climbing ordeal had
ended when Jim the instructor

finally got me to let go of the handholds and slowly let me down with the safety rope. Emily Fellows and her friends were hooting with laughter the whole time.

But how would *this* finish? With Mum calling the fire brigade and a fireman prising me off the tree? Or with me plummeting and crashing into the back garden with Mum shrieking and calling an ambulance?

My heart was thumping. I took a deep breath.

'Come on,' I muttered. 'You can do this. Keep going.'

I let go with my left hand, reached up, and grabbed onto the thick branch above my head. Then – very carefully – I moved my right foot up a few centimetres. Then my right hand to another branch. And in this way – very slowly – I hauled myself up the tree like some kind of gigantic hairless sloth. A sloth that was wearing a crash helmet and had an expression of sheer terror.

When I finally got to the top, Mum cheered, and I just couldn't stop grinning. Yes, I was still kind of terrified. But, also – I'd done it! This morning, just thinking about climbing Lofty had made my tummy all light and fluttery. And here I was, right at the top, about to grab the next clue!

I prised the small metal box from the branch. Now
that I was closer I could see that a piece of paper had
been sticky-taped to the outside:

Good job! You did it! Well done! (Warning:
Don't open this now – do it tomorrow morning.)

I slipped the box into my pocket and took in the view,
partly because I felt like I was on top of the world! And
partly because I was too terrified to move.

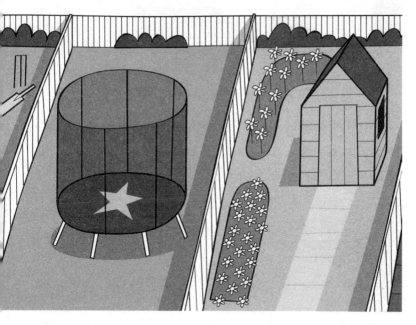

I could see everything from up here. I could even spy on the neighbours. The new couple next door had a veggie patch and a shed. The Ponting boys, next to them, had a football net, and a swing made out of a tyre, like the monkeys have at the zoo. Emily Fellows, three doors down, had a trampoline. It's a top-of-the-range one – I know this because she often boasts about it at school. And, next to the Fellows' place, on the corner, was Mr Pike's house.

Mr Pike is an old man in a wheelchair, who lives alone. He doesn't get out much. Emily Fellows tells scary stories about him – his house is definitely one you never visit at

Hallowe'en. But from up here I could see the flower bed in his back garden – neat rows of colourful flowers. It looked beautiful, but I'd heard that if you kicked a ball into his garden, he'd knife it and throw the punctured ball back. Pike the Spike, Emily Fellows calls him, and the name has caught on.

Beyond Mr Pike's house, I could see the whole town. From the ground it looks like nothing special, but from this high everything looked different. The duck pond was a shimmery silver oval. The museum, further away, was a huge grey brick-shaped building. And beyond it was a tree-covered hill – Harold's Peak, the highest point for miles around. It all looked . . . spectacular.

'Come on, Sausage!' Mum called up. 'You don't want to spend the rest of your birthday stuck up a tree, do you? I'm cooking your favourite for dinner!'

I took one last look around, and actually tingled with pride. I'd done it! I picked a small leaf from the top branch, as a memento, and carefully slipped it into my pocket. And then I edged slowly back to the ground. A monkey would have taken thirty seconds to get up and down, even if it had paused halfway to have a good scratch.

In the end it took me thirty *minutes* (with absolutely no scratching) to complete the second task.

As I jumped down from the lowest branch, I'd never been so happy to be back on the ground. I felt this incredible mix of relief and exhilaration and I couldn't stop grinning. It didn't matter how long it had taken me. Mum was clapping and cheering. Ernest was gurgling. Even Oates was barking his congratulations.

Or he might have spotted a cat again.

Later that evening, after my nans and granddads had phoned (with two enthusiastic but completely terrible versions of 'Happy Birthday to You'), the phone rang again, and I leapt up to answer it. It was Dad!

'Happy birthday, Princess!' he said.

Dad always calls me 'Princess' or 'Lolly', and Mum either calls me 'Chicken' or 'Sausage'. Don't they like my real name? They chose it!

Mum told me to put Dad on speakerphone, and when I did she said, 'So, you're trying to kill our daughter, are you?'

Dad chuckled.

'You're talking about the tree, I take it?'

35

'Yes, I'm talking about the tree,' Mum said. She seemed halfway between amused and annoyed. She often got that way with Dad. 'What's her task for tomorrow? Juggling chainsaws? Wrestling tigers? Tickling angry baboons?'

I couldn't help but giggle at this, though I was curious about the next task too, and a bit nervous. There were eight more to go, and nine days to do them in! Getting to the top of Lofty had been brilliant, but I'd had to work really hard to get there. What else did Dad have in store for me?

'Climbing is great,' he said. 'It's all about getting in touch with nature and overcoming your fears. I practically grew up in trees.'

'Like Tarzan?' I asked, completely impressed.

'No,' said Mum, 'Not at all like Tarzan. Your father grew up in a semi-detached on a posh housing estate.'

Dad chuckled again.

'Well, that's true. But we were climbing trees all the time, Lolly – me and your uncle Phil.' Phil is Dad's younger brother. 'There's adventure to be found in every back garden. Yes, we might have tumbled out a few times,' he admitted, 'but it never did us the least bit of harm.'

'That's what *you* think,' Mum said. 'A few bumps on the head would certainly explain a lot,' she added. 'About Uncle Phil, especially.'

'So, how are you all, anyway?' asked Dad, whose speciality was changing the subject. 'Has Ernest started playing the piano yet?'

Mum's speciality was being incredibly sarcastic. 'Yes,' she replied, 'he can't come to the phone right now – he's playing a concerto at the town hall.'

I could hear Dad laughing down the line.

Ernest, in fact, was on his hands and knees on his play mat, giving the tail of his toy dinosaur a very thorough chewing.

'What about you, Holly?' asked Dad. 'How are you?'

'I'm okay.'

'You managed to survive the tree, I take it?'

'Yep.'

'I knew you would. And you even survived kissing Mum?'

'Just about.'

'How was it?' he asked. 'Climbing Lofty, I mean. Not kissing Mum – I've done quite a lot of that.'

'Yuck.'

'So?' he asked.

'It was brilliant,' I said. 'Well, completely nerve-wracking. But at the top I could see everything – the whole town. It all looks so different from up high.'

'That's what mountain climbers say,' said Dad. 'The view is always worth the effort. I'm really proud of you, Holly. And Mum seems perfectly relaxed with the whole tree-climbing thing too,' he said. 'So everyone's happy.'

I laughed.

'Haven't you got an igloo to go to?' Mum said, rolling her eyes and trying to stop herself from smiling.

'Not an igloo,' said Dad.

'An ig?' I said.

Dad giggled.

'I'm actually staying in an ice hotel tonight. Which isn't as cold as it sounds. But I might not be spending quite as long on the toilet as usual.'

I laughed. So did Mum – she couldn't help it.

'What's the next task, Dad? Can you give me a clue?'

'Well, it's not juggling chainsaws,' he said. 'Or tickling baboons. Though when you see what it is, you might wish that it was. That's why I didn't want you to open it right away. You might have plummeted out of the tree.'

That night, I put the leaf I'd picked from Lofty into my adventure kit as a memento, and slipped the small metal box under my pillow, to open in the morning. Tomorrow was Thursday – a school day. But, much more importantly, it was also the day when I'd be attempting task number three.

4 Baking and Entering

In the morning, as soon as I woke up, I opened the little metal box, and inside was a folded-up piece of paper.

Task 3:
Bake something sweet, anything you like.
Then take it up the street as a gift for Mr Pike.

I gasped. Felt sick. *Mr Pike*, of all people. Pike the Spike! I'd wanted an *adventure*. Sledding with huskies, sleeping in igloos: they were proper adventures. Climbing Lofty was an actual adventure too. But cooking? Not an adventure. And delivering baked food to a terrifying old man – *that* seemed less like an adventure and more like a very weird nightmare.

Mum must have seen the look on my face as I walked into the kitchen.

'What's he making you do today?'

'Baking,' I said, glumly. 'I'm going to make a cake.'

'That's not *too* tricky,' she said encouragingly. 'Although I've got a fair idea who'll be wiping up the flour and picking up bits of eggshell from the floor.'

'Ernest?' I said.

'Guess again.'

'Anyway, making the cake isn't the hard bit,' I mumbled. 'I've got to deliver it too.'

'Oh?'

'To Mr Pike.'

She smiled broadly.

'It might be funny to you,' I said crossly, 'but Emily Fellows says that he's a knife-wielding kid-hater. And she lives next door to him, so she should know.'

'If Emily Fellows lived next door to me,' Mum said, 'I don't think I'd like children very much either.'

I guess Mum had a point.

'He's actually a nice man,' she said.

'Did you say "knife man"?'

She groaned.

'I said "*nice*". And if he's been a bit grumpy ever since Janet died – Mrs Pike – then who can blame him?'

'Being grumpy is one thing,' I said. 'Stabbing footballs – that's something else. I've made up my mind, Mum – I'm not going to do it. It's not a real adventure anyway.'

'Suit yourself,' she said. 'Though it's pretty strange how you can climb to the top of a really tall tree one day, conquering one of your biggest fears, and yet the very next day you're too chicken to take a cake to a neighbour.'

Then she made chicken noises. And did a little chicken dance. She even pretended to lay an egg, which was going a bit too far, I thought.

I grunted. Glared. But I had to admit, she did have a point. Plus, the task yesterday had been totally worth it – in the end – so maybe this one would be too.

Though I somehow doubted it.

As if the visit to Pike the Spike's house wasn't enough to worry about for one day, something happened at school that put me in an even worse mood.

'Artrageous' – the school art club – had been busy making posters for the talent show, and they'd pinned them up on noticeboards around the school overnight.

TALENT SHOW
Featuring…

Kool Beatz – hip-hop crew
Charlie Smith – piano
Harrison Duffy – comedy
Four-Mation – dance group
Holly Chambers – magic

The posters were suddenly everywhere I turned, each one featuring a different act. And, when I saw the poster nearest our classroom, I noticed that someone had already scribbled on it.

I heard giggles behind me.

Emily Fellows. Jade Skinner. The Harmer twins.

I swallowed. My face felt hot.

'Are you really magic?' Emily Fellows asked me. She said this in a sweet, sing-song voice, but her eyes were narrowed and mean. 'Are you a witch?'

I was trying to think of something clever or funny to say, but the words wouldn't come. It was like the rock-climbing again – my brain was scrambling, but my body – in this case, my mouth – had decided to shut down.

'Show us a trick, Holly,' she said in the same fake-sweet voice.

I shook my head.

'Make something disappear then,' she said. 'I know – make all your friends vanish.' Then she looked theatrically around. 'Oh, wait – they've already gone, in a puff of smoke.'

More giggling.

Emily Fellows' giggle is probably my least favourite sound in the entire world – it's like the laugh of an evil chipmunk.

She'd started hating me on the very first day of term, and it was over something completely stupid: she'd really wanted to be the class representative, but Ms Devenport gave the job to me instead. I'd grinned, and Emily thought that I was gloating – but I really wasn't – I was just happy to be chosen for something for a change.

But from that day on, she had it in for me – death stares, whispers, mean jokes – anything she could do to make my life a misery.

For example, when we were studying insects in science, I told Ms Devenport about how Oates is completely freaked out by flies. They make him really jumpy and he always tries to pounce on them, though he hasn't caught one yet. I noticed, as I was talking, that Emily was rolling her eyes, and I immediately felt horrible. Other times, she'd whisper, smirk or giggle about what I was saying. Her friends too. Any time I'd get an answer wrong in class – same thing. Soon, I couldn't say or do anything without being teased. So – mostly – I stopped.

Hardly ever put my hand up in class. Kept quiet in the lunch queue. In fact, I tried to keep quiet almost all of the time. Anything to avoid drawing attention to myself.

As I was staring sadly at the talent-show poster, with the girls still sniggering behind me, Asha Chopra walked over to me.

Asha is gentle and smiley, and she wears gold bangles that chime like tiny cymbals as she walks. We used to be good friends. We didn't fall out or anything, but she just sits with other people at lunch now, and I mostly sit by myself.

'You all right?' she asked.

I nodded, but I was trying really, really hard not to cry.

'I wish I had a talent,' she said, looking at the poster. And I was thinking, *Me too.*

All I wanted to do was go home and lie on my bed and just sob. But instead, I had a cake to bake and a crazy old man to visit.

Before school I'd found a recipe for an 'easy chocolate cake' on the internet and printed it off. It would be the first cake I'd ever baked, and for a stranger too! When we got home, Mum had already put the ingredients out on the kitchen bench, and all the utensils – measuring cups, scales, bowls and the cake tin. I know she was only trying to help, but I was really annoyed that she'd got all the stuff out – I could easily have done that myself. This was *my* task, *my* adventure, and I wanted to show Mum and Dad how grown up I was. While I was washing my hands, Mum was hovering behind me.

'I'm okay,' I said. 'I don't need your help, thanks.'

'I thought I'd just monitor.'

'I'm good, really.'

'In case you had any questions.'

'I don't.'

'I won't get in your way, I just want to make sure that you don't burn the house down. Or poison Mr Pike.'

She was trying to be funny, but I really needed some space, so I glared at her, and she seemed to get the point.

'Okay, okay,' she said. 'Give me a shout if you —'

'Mum!'

Finally she ducked out of the kitchen and went into the living room to play with Ernest. Oates stayed with me, no doubt hoping for scraps. He was in luck. Mum was right about the mess. Within minutes it was foggy with clouds of flour, and cake mixture was splattered everywhere. It looked like someone had let a monkey loose in a bakery.

After an hour and a half, though, I'd actually done it: mixed the batter, put it in the oven and watched it rise. It didn't look perfect, but it was round, at least, and kind of the right colour. It smelled pretty good too. When it had cooled down a bit, I spread on the chocolate icing and – the best bit – licked the spoon.

Finally, I stepped back and grinned with satisfaction. I'd baked my first-ever cake!

But of course the frightening part of the task was yet to come.

I don't think I've ever walked more slowly than I did on my way to Mr Pike's place. I went up to his house the same way that someone might approach a grizzly bear's cave. Except that I was carrying a cake (which would be a really stupid idea when visiting a bear of any kind).

Despite what Mum had said, I just couldn't shake the image of a knife-wielding maniac spiking footballs for fun.

Mr Pike's house is at the corner of our street. It's small and plain-looking, with a flat concrete front yard and an iron gate that creaked when I opened it, like something out of a horror movie.

I knocked on his door – gently, hoping that the old

man was either out or that he wouldn't hear me. If he didn't answer the door, I could take the cake home, stuff my face with it in front of the telly and email Dad to ask him for the next task. But as soon as I'd knocked I heard an impatient shout.

'Who's there?'

I was too scared to answer. I could hear the buzz of his electric wheelchair coming up the hall. Next, there was the sound of him grunting as he unlocked the front door – two heavy, clunky locks. Then he flung the door open and squinted up at me for a few moments.

Mr Pike was a smallish man with grey side-parted hair, bushy eyebrows and a good-sized nose.

'Yes?' he said, grumpily.

The only word I could force out was, 'Cake.'

He looked at the cake, then at me, then back at the cake.

'What?' he said, frowning.

'I'm Holly,' I said – squeaked, almost. 'From four doors down?'

'Ah,' he said, and seemed to soften – a bit. He coughed. 'Holly Chambers, if I am not mistaken.'

I nodded.

'I've been expecting you,' he said. Which, as everyone knows, is the kind of thing that baddies in movies say just before they start torturing the hero. I wanted to turn and run back home but, not for the first time, I froze in panic.

'Well, don't just stand there, young lady, letting all the cold air in. Enter, enter.'

I found just enough courage to step inside, close the door behind me and follow him as he motored down the gloomy hall. He pointed me into the living room and told me to take a seat while he 'fetched something from the kitchen'.

I put the cake on the polished wooden table by the big window, sat in one of the two old brown armchairs and glanced around the room. There was an old telly in the corner and an old-fashioned radio with a dial. Framed pictures on the walls. A large bookcase, crammed with books. It was – cosy. A person who lived in a place like this couldn't be too horrible, could they?

But through the window I could see his back garden, and the big colourful flowerbed – the flowerbed where balls came to die.

When I heard the buzz of the electric wheelchair again, I turned.

Mr Pike was coming this way – grasping a huge knife!

My mouth opened but the scream got stuck in my throat.

'You'll sample a piece of your cake with me, won't you?' he said. He smiled, and it didn't *seem* like the crazy smile of a deranged murderer. So I took a deep breath and nodded.

With two small plates balanced on his lap, he went to the table, cut two thick slices of cake, put them on the plates, and handed one to me.

'Still warm,' he said and, after he'd taken a bite, added, 'Very flavourful. Did you make it yourself?'

I nodded. My breathing had slowed down by now – a bit. I nibbled my piece of cake, and he was right. It was actually okay. I felt a tiny wave of pride. And I felt a lot less nervous now that he was no longer gripping the knife. Plus, seeing Mr Pike up close – and the inside of his house with all its books and pictures – made him seem much less frightening.

'So, how is your adventure going?' he asked. 'Your father explained what he was up to, and I must say it sounds like tremendous fun.'

I nodded again, though it had so far been less 'tremendous fun' and more 'completely terrifying'.

'I love an adventure myself,' he said. 'Though, nowadays, because of these –' he pointed to his legs – 'most of my adventures have to be inside here.' He pointed to his head. 'But that's not so bad, because I have help, you see. I can still travel around the world.

And travel in time too – into the past and into the future.'

I frowned. Maybe Emily Fellows was right, maybe Mr Pike *was* crazy.

'A time machine?' I said.

'In a way,' he said, smiling. 'I read lots of books. Each one takes you on a journey, does it not?'

He buzzed over to the bookcase and pulled out an old book: a dark blue cover, with gold writing. 'Whenever I'm reading this, for example, I'm ten years old again. And that is a very nice age to be.' He showed me the cover – it said *The Adventures of Tom Sawyer.* 'Have you read it?'

I shook my head.

'In that case,' he said, handing it to me, 'it's yours.'

As we ate our pieces of cake, he fired questions at me: how many tasks I'd done (three, now), how many more were to go (seven), where my dad was (Sweden, I said, or possibly Denmark), and what my baby brother was like (very loud and very dribbly).

'Your father also mentioned that you're interested in magic,' said Mr Pike.

I nodded. Blushed.

'And have you performed, I wonder, in front an audience?'

'Not yet,' I said. 'But I've got the school talent show in a week's time.'

'Marvellous,' he said, but I was thinking how completely un-marvellous it was going to be.

Then Mr Pike said that if I wanted to practise my magic act before the talent show, he'd be honoured to help. I tried to say no but he was really persistent.

'You can't do a big show without a proper rehearsal,' he said. 'Come here on Saturday morning. Ten o'clock sharp. Bring your tricks. I'll call your mother to let her know.'

'Okay,' I said reluctantly. Then: 'I'd better be off now.'

He showed me to the door.

'Thank you so much for the delicious cake,' he said.

I smiled, and said, 'Wait – do you have a clue for me? The next task?'

'It's in there,' he said, pointing to the book that I was clutching. 'Good luck on your adventures, Holly. See you on Saturday.'

5 The Amazing Mysterio

'So, you managed to survive, did you?' said Mum as I arrived home.

If anything, she became even more sarcastic when my dad was away, as if she had to provide enough sarcasm for two adults.

I grunted, and ran upstairs.

In my room, I put the chocolate-cake recipe in my adventure-kit-shoebox, next to the leaf I'd picked from Lofty.

Then I sat on my bed and opened the book that Mr Pike had given me. I wondered if I'd have to read the whole thing to work out the next clue or task, but when I turned to Chapter One, a piece of paper fell to the floor. I picked it up and read my dad's familiar handwriting.

Task 4:
Follow these tracks,
You'll hear lots of these.
It's a bit of a test
So you might need (this).

I stared at the clue for the longest time.

The tracks looked very strange. I knew what *dogs'* paw prints were like from the millions of times that Oates had trodden mud into the house. But animal tracks weren't something I knew much about. Animal *poo*, however, I was a complete expert in. Seriously. Just after Ernest was born I'd been complaining a lot about the pong of his nappies, and Dad bought me a card game called 'Plop Trumps', as a joke. The cards had photos of animal poo on them, complete with random facts, and Dad and I had played it so much that now I could identify the droppings of pretty much every animal. But their tracks, not so much. And the rest of the clue was incredibly confusing too. It didn't even rhyme.

When Dad was having trouble thinking of something to write, he usually got up and took Oates for a walk, or had a little chat with me or Mum, or even Ernest. He said that this often helped to 'work his ideas loose'. So I thought it was worth a try for me.

Ernest was having a nap, and Oates was sleeping too, so I went to see Mum. She was taking advantage of the quiet to do some cleaning. She'd tidied the kitchen (she was right, I had left it in a bit of a mess) and now she'd moved on to the bathroom. When I walked in, she was scrubbing the toilet bowl.

'Yuck,' I said.

She turned to me, rolled her eyes, and said, 'How do you think the loo gets cleaned, Holly? Do you think we get a weekly visit from the toilet-cleaning fairy? You know – the tooth fairy's unlucky little sister – she puts on a tiny fairy wetsuit and swims up the U-bend and . . .'

'I get it, Mum,' I said, with a sigh.

She smiled.

'What's that in your hand? The next clue?'

I nodded.

'Read it out then.'

I did, and she looked as baffled as I was.

'What do you think it means?' I asked.

'It means,' she replied, 'that your father is a genuine nutcase.' She smiled again. 'Show me the tracks.'

I did. She shrugged.

'Could those be webbed feet?' she said, with a shrug. I wasn't sure, but the word 'web' had given me a great idea.

'The internet!' I said. 'I'll search for animal tracks!'

I left Mum scrubbing the loo, dashed to the computer, and it wasn't long before I'd found what I was looking for.

Mum was right. Ducks.

And when I read the clue again, it actually made sense now. It *did* rhyme after all:

Follow these tracks,
You'll hear lots of quacks
It's a bit of a test
So you might need . . .

To be dressed? A vest? Who knew, but at least I'd figured out the first mystery.

I went to tell Mum what I'd discovered. She'd moved on to the shower by now, with a different scrubbing brush in her hand.

'The shower-head fairy hasn't been recently either,' she said. 'So I thought I'd better do it myself.'

'Ducks,' I said, ignoring her. 'They're duck tracks. I think the next clue's by the duck pond.'

'Nice one,' she said. 'We can go tomorrow, after school, if you like.'

'We? It's *my* adventure, Mum. Adventurers don't bring their mums along.'

She frowned, shook her head.

'You were happy to let me go to Mr Pike's by myself,' I said. 'What's the difference?'

'He only lives four houses up the street,' she said.

'The pond's ten minutes' walk away, and you have to cross two busy roads to get there.' She waggled her head, as if going through the route in her mind. 'Three, actually.'

'I can cross roads,' I said. 'We did a thing at school. With Horatio the Road Safety Hedgehog. Look left, look right, look left again. Walk, don't run.'

'You're nine years old,' Mum said.

'Ten.'

'True,' she said. 'Sorry. But the answer's still "no", I'm afraid.'

I groaned. 'You told me once that when you were a kid you basically used to roam the streets and only come home when it started getting dark.'

'It was a different time then, Holly.'

'How was it different?'

'It just was.'

I sighed, and then stomped off to my room. Well, actually, I didn't stomp, because I didn't want to wake Ernest and get into trouble. But I really felt like stomping. *And* slamming the door of my room. Which I also didn't do. I *was* incredibly grumpy though. Because my dad had planned all these adventures for me, but my mum seemed determined to stop them.

When the phone rang that evening, I was in the front room, practising my magic: the card trick and the rope trick. The card trick was okay, but the rope trick I kept fumbling.

Mum was in Ernest's room trying to 'settle him off'. That wasn't going at all well either, judging by Mum's sighs and Ernest's screams.

I answered the phone. It was Dad. He asked me straight away how the Dadventure was going, but I wasn't really in the mood for talking.

'It's going okay,' I said.

'What task are you up to?'

'I did number three today.'

'Aha! Well done! And was it fun?'

'Kind of.'

'Did you tidy the kitchen after?'

'Kind of.'

'Does "kind of" mean "no"?'

'Kind of.'

Dad giggled. He had a great giggle. I usually loved it when I made him laugh, but right now it just made me miss him even more.

'How was Mr Pike?' he asked.

'All right.'

'Just "all right"?'

'He was actually nice,' I said.

'Funny, eh?'

'He wasn't *funny*, exactly.'

'No – I mean, it's funny, isn't it, that sometimes things that might seem really scary turn out to be not-at-all-scary in the end?'

'Yeah,' I said.

'Do you know why I chose him for the cake?' Dad asked.

'Because you wanted to completely freak me out?' I guessed.

'Well, maybe a tiny bit. But there was another reason too.'

'You thought it might be nice for him to have a visitor?'

'Nope. Well, partly, yes,' he admitted, 'but there was

another reason, too – a really good one. All of the tasks are for a reason in fact. Did he tell you that he used to be a magician?'

'No.'

'Called himself "The Amazing Mysterio". Presumably because it sounded a lot more magical than "Reg Pike".'

'Are you pulling my leg?'

'No,' he said. 'You can ask Mum. He was good too. His wife, Janet, was his assistant. He used to make her disappear. I asked him once if he could teach me how to do it with Mum.'

'I'm telling her you said that.'

This made him giggle again, and then he changed the subject.

'Did you work out the next clue yet?'

'I think so. It's at the duck pond, isn't it?'

'I can neither confirm nor deny that.'

'*Dad.*'

'Okay,' he said, 'you're right, Smartypants.'

'Good,' I said, but I was still feeling a bit glum, and Dad could obviously tell.

'What's wrong, Lolly?'

'It's just . . . Mum won't let me go to the duck pond on my own.'

'Oh.'

'She says it's too dangerous.'

There was a moment of silence.

'Well, if she says that,' Dad said, 'then she must be right. Mum knows best.'

Now it was my turn to be quiet.

'I'm off to the airport later,' he said, changing the subject again. 'Flying to Greenland, where I'll be a deer-herd for three days. There's no mobile phone reception. So I won't be able to call.'

'A deer-herd?' I said.

'Like a shepherd. But with deer.'

'So you get to hang about with Rudolph, but I'm not even allowed to visit ducks without being supervised?'

'What do you call a deer with no eyes?' Dad said.

I groaned and said, 'No eye deer.' Dad often tried to snap me out of bad moods by making jokes. It used to work when I was seven or eight, but these days it wasn't nearly so successful.

'What do you call a *fish* with no eyes?' he said, and I'd

actually never heard that one before. 'A fsh!' he said. 'Get it? "Fsh" – a fish with no "i"s!'

'I got it,' I said. 'It just wasn't very funny.'

Except it was, actually. Funny. I just wasn't ready to come out of my grumpy mood yet.

'You just told me that every task in the Dadventure is there for a reason,' I said.

'Yes.'

'So – why the duck pond?'

He hesitated.

'That one was for me, really,' he said.

'Huh?'

'I've been all around the world, Lolly. In jungles, deserts, up mountains, down rivers. But none of that was nearly as exciting as taking you to the duck pond when you were little. Watching you with the ducks – it was brilliant. Some of the happiest times of my life.'

I went quiet – smiled, blushed.

Then Dad peppered me with loads of questions – about school, about the treasure hunt, about my preparations for the talent show, about Mum, about Ernest.

Ernest, by this time, had stopped crying at last, and Mum came into the front room looking worn out and just about ready to be 'settled off' herself.

I said goodbye to Dad – 'Love you times a gazillion,' he said – and then I handed the phone to Mum.

She went into their bedroom and talked to Dad for a really long time.

I don't know what they talked about, but I do know

that, when she hung up, Mum sat down next to me and said that I was allowed to go to the duck pond with Oates, but with no human supervision, if that's what I really wanted.

I gave her a hug, a real bone-cruncher.

6   The Duck Pond

The next day was Friday. School was surprisingly okay.
At lunch, I sat at a table with Asha and Jaya, Jack B and
Jack C. The Dadventure seemed to have given me a bit
of confidence back. If I could climb a tall tree and visit a
scary old man (who turned out to be not-at-all-scary),
then I could definitely try to be a bit more sociable at
school. We talked about places that we'd visited – Asha
has been to India. She has a grandma there, and that, I
thought, was almost as cool as having an explorer for
a dad. Talking to Asha and her friends was so nice that
I managed to ignore most of the teasing from Emily
Fellows and her gang.

Then, after school, Oates and I set off for the duck

pond. Mum, looking extremely worried, watched us cross the first road, and then she went back inside the house.

The second street we came to wasn't busy, so we crossed straight away, but the third road was another story. I asked Oates to sit while we waited for a break in the traffic, but he just sniffed my shoes instead.

Mum says that Oates has selective hearing. Like, he can hear a can of dog food being opened from the other side of town, but ask him to do something like 'sit' or 'come here', and he'll completely ignore you. I don't blame him though. I use the same tactic myself, when it's time to brush my teeth or change Ernest's nappy.

When we finally crossed the last road and got to the park, Oates started tugging on his lead and barking loudly. *He* obviously wanted an adventure too, and an adventure for Oates usually means chasing something, exploring, or sniffing other dogs' bottoms. Mum and Dad always let him off his lead in places like this, but I just couldn't risk it. It would be really hard for me to get him back if he ran off. So, as we walked up to the pond, I gripped his lead very tightly indeed.

Dad and I used to come here loads when I was little.

Other people would throw stale bread to the ducks, but not us. Dad said that if ducks were meant to eat bread, they'd have built their own windmills and bakeries. Bread gives ducks stomach ache, he said. So we'd just sit on the bench facing the pond and watch them paddle and quack and dive for food.

But this time, of course, it wasn't the ducks I was here for – so we padded around the pond, searching for the next clue. Well, *I* was searching for it, at least. Oates was barking randomly and stopping every few seconds to sniff a clump of grass or do a wee.

When we'd finally made it all the way around the pond, I'd found nothing (except for a duck feather, which I put in my pocket for the adventure box). I was feeling tired and incredibly grumpy by now. So we went over to the bench – the same one that me and Dad used to sit on – and I sat down and tried to think. Oates was sniffing under the bench. He'd probably got the scent of another dog's wee, or something equally disgusting.

I thought about the clue again: I hadn't even worked out the second part of it, yet. 'It's a bit of a test, so you might need (this)'. What could 'this' be? The answer came to me like a jolt of electricity, whooshing up my body and forcing out a gasp.

'It's a bit of a test, so you might need a *rest*.'

This bench!

I leapt up and looked all around it. Nothing. So I lay on my back on the ground and shuffled underneath.

A clue! Sticky-taped to the underside! I ripped it off. And that's when I let go of the lead. Only for a second, but that's all that Oates needed.

He was off like a greyhound, trailing the lead behind him. By the time I'd scrambled out from under the bench and got to my feet, he was already halfway across the field. I chased after him but he was getting further and further away, and then he disappeared behind a dip. I had a horrible, sick feeling – he was heading for the bushes and, beyond them, the busy road. My heart was thumping. I sprinted as fast as I could.

When I finally caught sight of him, this huge feeling of relief overwhelmed me. It made my legs wobble. Oates hadn't run into traffic. He hadn't even got as far as the bushes. In fact, he'd come to a complete stop, right next to Mum, who had Ernest in his pushchair.

I jogged over to them, but by the time I'd got there I'd gone from feeling incredibly relieved to really, furiously annoyed.

'You followed me! You said you wouldn't!'

'I just happened to be in the area,' Mum said, shrugging unconvincingly. 'Ernest fancied a walk.'

I gave her a look.

'Okay,' she admitted. 'I just couldn't stand it at home. With you out here. So I thought I'd try and look out for you but stay out of sight. That way I could stop worrying and you could still have an adventure.'

'You were snooping on me,' I said angrily. 'Like a spy.'

She shook her head. 'I was snooping on you like a mum,' she said. 'It's completely different.'

We stood in silence for a while, though Oates was panting and Ernest was gurgling.

'Did you find the clue?' asked Mum.

I grunted, 'Yes.'

'Brilliant,' she said. 'And Oates found me, so I suppose you're both winners.'

She was trying to be funny, but I wasn't in the mood. Real adventurers don't have their mums hiding in the background.

We walked home in silence. I was too annoyed to speak, and Ernest fell asleep. Even Oates was quiet (though he still stopped now and again to spray a bit of wee up walls and trees and lampposts. How much wee could one medium-sized dog have?)

Then Mum broke the silence.

'So, what *is* the next clue, anyway?'

I hadn't even looked at it. I'd just scrunched it into my

fist in all the commotion, and that's where it still was. I opened my hand, uncrumpled the paper and read it out loud.

Task 5:
Well done! And now for your next mission: Search for a picture of your first expedition.

'My first expedition?' I repeated breathlessly. 'When was that?'

Mum gave it some thought.

'We went for a week at the seaside when you were two.'

'A beach holiday's hardly an expedition, Mum,' I pointed out.

'With Dad,' she said, '*every* holiday's an expedition. We explored caves. Took the metal detector and searched the beach for treasure.'

'And we've got photos?'

'Yep. There's an entire album of that holiday, I think.

Parents tend to go crazy like that with their first kid. Sorry, Ernest,' she said, but Ernest was still asleep.

I tried to think where that photo album might be.

'Is it in Dad's "filing system"?' I asked.

Mum smiled and nodded, and I smiled back. I was already halfway through my tasks, and now I knew where to find clue number six.

7 The First Expedition

At Uncle Phil's house, he's got this cool digital photo frame in the kitchen: the photo changes every few seconds (although most them seem to be of Uncle Phil doing something completely daft).

We don't have one of those. Our photos never ever change. In the front room, on the wall, there's a picture of Mum and Dad on their wedding day, with big smiles and old-fashioned hairstyles, and there's another one of Mum on a beach – wearing a dress, on white sand, with a sand dune and a deep blue sky behind her. There are photos of my grandparents from when they were only *quite* old, and a few of me from when I was cute.

The rest of our photos are in albums in the loft. My dad puts pretty much everything up there, in cardboard boxes. Mum calls it 'Dad's filing system'. There are boxes of old clothes, boxes of Dad's old notebooks and boxes of all our Christmassy stuff.

I used to be nervous about climbing up there, but after task two the loft ladder suddenly seemed like nothing to worry about.

At the top of the ladder, I pushed open the trapdoor, hoisted myself up into the loft and began to crawl around. It was dusty and smelled of old books, and there were lots of cardboard boxes, including one that my dad

had helpfully labelled 'photo albums'. I sat cross-legged next to it, reached in, and pulled out an album.

The first one was old, but the faded photos were mostly of a girl who looked strangely familiar. Then I realised – she looked just like me! Except it wasn't me, because the clothes were really old-fashioned. It took me a few moments to work it out – it was Mum, when she was my age. On a rope swinging across a stream. Building a campfire. Riding a bike that seemed two sizes too big for her – and with no helmet either. All things that I wouldn't be allowed to do, at least not without serious safety equipment and an ambulance on standby.

The next album was the one I'd been looking for. The first picture was of a very young me, on the beach, trying to outstare a crab. I tucked the album under one arm, climbed carefully down the ladder and then ran downstairs to the living room.

Oates was sleeping on the carpet, completely spread out, like a rug but with added snoring. Mum was on the sofa with a cup of tea, looking exhausted too. It was hard to imagine that she'd once been that full-of-beans girl I'd just seen in those photos.

'Can I look too?' she asked, so I sat next to her and opened the album.

Mum laughed at the first picture.

'You wanted to take that crab home and keep it as a pet,' she said. 'Maybe we *should* have – might have been less trouble than certain dogs I could mention.'

As if on cue, Oates farted in his sleep. We both burst out laughing.

I turned page after page, hoping to find the next clue stuck to a photo or tucked behind one. But there was nothing and, when we'd finished, I looked at Mum and said, 'Are you sure this was my first holiday? There wasn't one before it?'

She shook her head.

'When you were a newborn, Dad had to go to Morocco for a week, for a magazine job. He wanted us to join him, but I wouldn't allow it. Too dangerous. You were too young.'

I rolled my eyes. It all sounded very familiar: Dad planning something adventurous, and Mum being the fun police.

Then she exclaimed, 'Aha!'

It woke Oates up. He jumped to his feet and looked around, flustered.

Mum was pointing to a photo on the wall: the one of her standing on a beach. She was grown up in the photo, but younger. And she wasn't in a bikini or anything – instead she was wearing clothes.

'That's you at the beach,' I said, puzzled. 'But I'm not even there.'

'It's not a beach,' she said, smiling. 'It's the Sahara Desert. Your dad took the photo.'

'But the clue was about *me*,' I said. '*My* first expedition.'

'It was on that day,' said Mum, '– just a few hours after that photo had been taken – that I discovered something incredible.'

'What?'

'I was pregnant, Holly.'

'Huh?'

'With you. Your first expedition,' she added, 'was before you were even born.'

I'd seen that photo every day for pretty much my whole life, yet I'd never realised where it was taken – or that I was actually in it (sort of). Sometimes you just don't notice the things that are right under your nose.

I jumped up from the sofa, past Oates, and lifted the photo off the wall. And there, sure enough, stuck to the back of the frame, was the next clue.

8   Worms

Task 6:
0738336311 + 7 + 12 + 23

'Maths?' I said, frowning at Mum in the living room. 'Can I borrow your phone, please?'

Mum handed it to me and I used the calculator, hoping that the answer to the sum would mean something.

738,336,353.

Nothing.

Then I had a thought: had Dad come up with a number that, when upside down, spelled a word?

Harrison Duffy does this with a calculator in maths – he writes 58008 and then flips it upside down to spell 'BOOBS', which he seems to find completely hilarious, every single time.

My dad's number, however, doesn't seem to spell anything.

I was about to pass the phone back to Mum when I had another thought: that first number – could that be a phone number?

I asked Mum for permission to call, and then, very carefully, dialled.

I was right! It was ringing! I could hardly breathe – halfway between super-excited and heart-stoppingly nervous.

'Wok Around the Clock. How can I help you?'

I panicked and pressed the red 'end call' button, stared at Mum and said breathlessly, 'It's the Chinese takeaway.' And then, I realised. 'Those other numbers must be things on the menu!'

Mum couldn't stop herself from chuckling.

I dashed to the kitchen drawer where we kept all the takeaway menus, and pulled out the Chinese one.

7 was hot-and-sour soup

12 was salt-and-pepper tofu

23 was deep-fried calamari tentacles.

Eek! All things that I'd never tried. Also never, ever wanted to try.

Back in the living room, I was shaking my head.

'What *was* Dad thinking?' I muttered.

'He was probably thinking that your tastebuds could do with an adventure too, Holly. There's more to life than spaghetti Bolognese and chicken nuggets, you know.' She could see that I was about to protest, so she added, 'I didn't really feel like cooking tonight anyway. We'll order those new things and a couple of old favourites, too – special fried rice and prawn crackers. Yum. What do you say to that?'

I shrugged. I wasn't at all looking forward to the new food, but fried rice was always a treat, and the thought of finishing three tasks in one day was pretty awesome.

So I called up the number again to order the food. The voice on the other end of the phone belonged to Gary – Gary Chan, Dad's friend from school. Gary has never even *been* to China, according to Dad, but he learned how to cook the food from his mum, and he's really, really good at it.

I gave Gary the order and, when he asked for our name and address at the end of the call, he said, 'Ah, Holly, I thought it was you. Your dad told me to expect a special order from you soon. He also asked me to give you a message.'

'Oh?'

'Yes – the message is "Good luck!"'

An hour later, I was piling my plate with spoonfuls of fried rice and some prawn crackers, and wrinkling my nose at the new dishes. Across the table from me, Ernest was in his high chair next to Mum, and Oates was under the table waiting impatiently for something delicious to hit the floor.

The hot-and-sour soup, in a plastic tub, was a blood-coloured liquid with bits of meat and tiny prawns and swirly bits of egg all through it. Yuck! And the calamari looked even more disgusting: a metal tray of lumpy, fat brown worms. Only the tofu looked even slightly appetising – golden cubes, like big, fried dice.

Mum reached out with her chopsticks, expertly picked up a cube of tofu and popped it into her mouth. I looked at her, warily. 'Mmm,' she said, after she'd chewed and swallowed it. 'It's actually really, really good.'

I took a deep breath, stabbed a cube with my fork and sniffed it as if it might be poisoned, before finally taking a medium-sized bite. Mum was – incredibly – right. It was crunchy and tangy on the outside, but soft and melty on the inside. I finished the cube and then had another one straight away. Mum grinned, impressed. And then she reached out and trapped a piece of calamari between her chopsticks – it looked like it might wriggle away at any moment.

'What's calamari, anyway?'

'Squid,' she said. I pulled a face.

'As in, little octopuses?'

'Kind of,' she said, and then she chewed on her piece as if there was nothing at all weird about putting a tentacle in your mouth. I grimaced just watching her, but she was making one of those faces that grown-ups do when their mouth is full but the thing that they're eating is really delicious.

So I found the smallest tentacle in the container, pinched it between a finger and thumb, closed my eyes and, grimacing, put the entire thing into my mouth. Then I chewed. I was expecting something rubbery and gristly, but it was surprisingly soft – and delicious!

Mum was grinning her head off at my reaction.

'Brilliant,' she said.

I had another piece, and some fried rice and prawn

crackers. Then it was time to brave the hot-and-sour soup.

Mum sampled it first.

'It's a bit on the spicy side,' she said, 'but not too bad. You should be able to cope.'

But I shouldn't have listened to her – Mum always goes for the vindaloo when we have Indian takeaway: she *loves* chilli.

I took just one spoonful – that was all.

I'm not sure about the 'sour' bit, but they weren't joking about the 'hot' part – 'hot' as in 'incredibly spicy', as in 'someone's just set fire to my tongue'. I leapt up, dashed to the fridge with my tongue hanging out like Oates's, poured a glass of water and drank it in one, but it didn't put the fire out. Not even close.

'Water won't work,' Mum said. 'You need milk.' She went to the fridge and poured me a glass, and it worked – a bit. My tongue was still tingling, and my lips. I was panting.

Mum had seemed slightly concerned at first, and a bit guilty, but now she was snorting with laughter. Even Ernest was giggling, and Oates had got up to see what all the commotion was about.

'Good job, you,' Mum said, when everyone – and my mouth – had finally calmed down. 'You did it.'

'But where's the next clue?' I said. 'Gary's message was "good luck", but that can't be the clue, can it?'

I looked under the foil containers, but there were no pieces of paper stuck to the bottom, and the white plastic bag that the food had come in was empty except for a single fortune cookie, which I picked out.

'Only one?' I said. Mum raised her eyebrows, and a smile slowly spread across her face.

'You know another word for "luck", don't you?' she said.

My eyes widened.

'Fortune,' I said, and snapped the cookie open.

Inside was a tiny slip of paper, which said:

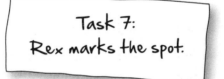

Task 7:
Rex marks the spot.

9   The Rehearsal

On Saturday morning, at ten o'clock, I was sitting in Mr Pike's living room, in the same armchair as before. He was in his electric wheelchair, facing me.

'And how is the treasure hunt going, young lady?'

'All right,' I said. 'I'm up to number seven already. Except now I'm a bit stuck.'

'Oh?'

'The clue is "Rex marks the spot".'

'And do you know anyone called Rex?' he asked.

'No, and neither does Mum.'

We'd been through all of this last night. When Ernest had gone to sleep and I'd put the duck feather, a spare set of chopsticks, and the photo of me and the crab into the adventure kit, Mum asked me back to the table. I'd thought she was going to make me clean up, but instead she told me to sit down, and then taught me how to use chopsticks. We practised with salted peanuts. It was fun – trying to pick them out of one bowl and move them to another. It was really tricky though, especially since I was also trying to work out the meaning of 'Rex marks the spot' the whole time.

I had no success at all with the clue, and only slightly more luck with the peanuts – most of them pinged onto the floor for Oates to gobble up. After the chopsticks game it was time for bed, and I lay there, wide awake, trying to work out the clue.

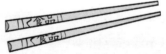

'Rex sounds like a dog's name,' said Mr Pike, on Saturday morning.

'But I don't know any dogs called that either.'

'It's also Latin for "king",' he said. 'Now, do you happen to know any kings, I wonder?'

I shook my head, and we both smiled, but then we sat in awkward silence until he nodded at the plastic bag beside me, rubbed his hands together and said, 'So, are you going to show me any tricks?'

I shrugged. 'Maybe . . . You didn't tell me you're a magician.'

'You didn't ask. Besides, I'm an ex-magician. I hung up my top hat a long time ago.'

'Why?'

He shrugged. 'I'm getting on a bit now, Holly – and it's rather hard to do magic when you're sitting down the whole time.'

I fished the pack of cards from my bag.

'Can you show me a trick?' I said.

'I'm a bit rusty,' he said. But he took the cards from me, and the way he handled them was completely mesmerising – shuffling, riffling and fanning, it was like his hands and the cards were doing a dance together. Then he put the deck on his lap, took the top card – the three of spades – and spun it around in his hand, between his fingers. And then . . . it disappeared.

It was in his hand – and then it wasn't.

And then, with another flourish, it was back. I actually gasped and shook my head in wonder.

'How did you *do* that?'

'Practice,' he said.

'If I was even half as good at something as that – I'd never give up.'

He smiled sheepishly.

'Your turn,' he said. But now I was more nervous than ever. Apart from the audition for the talent show, which was only in front of Mrs Stanley, who is super-nice, I'd only ever done magic for my family before – and Mum and Dad clap at absolutely everything. If Oates catches a biscuit in his mouth, for example, or actually sits when you ask him to, he gets a round of applause. If Ernest burps, they give him a standing ovation. So doing magic for them was no problem. Doing tricks in front of an actual magician, and a brilliant one too – *that* was something else completely.

The trick was usually an easy one, but not today. I fumbled the cards and got my words muddled up. When I'd finished, he smiled and said, 'Not bad. Not bad at all. But you were rushing it a little. Nerves?'

I nodded, blushing.

'Pass me the cards,' he said, and then, without needing to ask how I'd done it, performed the same trick, except that his version was about a million times better. He slowed it down, and seemed to be looking into my eyes instead of at the pack, as if he was actually reading my mind to find the identity of each card. A couple of times, he pretended to get muddled up – 'Is it the ten – no, no, wait – the *nine* of hearts?' Then he whispered, 'Let the audience think that you're about to mess up, and then – bam! – you get it right.' He handed me the cards. 'Your turn.'

So I did the trick again, and I was still a bit shaky, but it felt much better, especially when he said, 'Bravo.'

'Why *did* you give up?' I asked him. He chuckled. 'I'm serious,' I said. 'You're completely amazing at magic.'

'I'll take the compliment.'

'It's not a compliment,' I said. It was – but it wasn't. I just couldn't believe that he had that talent, but kept it hidden from the world.

He hesitated, smiled.

'We were a team,' he said. 'Me and Janet – my wife. The Amazing Mysterio and The Enchanting Shakira. Since she died, I just can't face it – going back on stage without her. It wouldn't feel right.' Then he glanced at his watch. 'We better get going, Holly, or we'll be late.'

'Late?'

'The key to success in show business,' he said, 'is punctuality.'

'Late for what?'

'For your rehearsal.'

'But we're having it now, aren't we?'

He smiled.

'Performing in front of one person,' he said, 'hardly

counts as a proper *rehearsal*. Not when you're due to perform in front of a huge crowd next week.'

'Don't remind me.'

'So you're booked to appear at the old people's home, in exactly half an hour.'

My chest suddenly felt incredibly tight, like the breath was being squeezed out of me, and for a second I froze. Then I said the first excuse that came into my head. 'I can't do it – my mum needs me home.'

He shook his head. 'I told her about it on the phone,' he explained. 'She said it would be a good adventure for you – her words exactly.'

When I'd left the house, Mum had said, 'Knock 'em dead, Holly. Not literally.' I'd given her a confused look, but now it suddenly made sense.

Mr Pike must have seen the panic in my eyes.

'Look,' he said, 'it won't be a big audience – just a few people – and they'll be incredibly grateful for any kind of entertainment that isn't bingo – trust me. The only downside,' he added, tapping his chair, 'is that you're unlikely to get a standing ovation.'

As we left the house, I glanced at Emily Fellows'

place next door, to make sure that she hadn't seen us together. I felt ashamed for checking – but I knew that, if she spotted me with Mr Pike, the news would be all round the class first thing on Monday morning, and I really didn't need anything new to be teased about.

It didn't take us long to get to the old people's home. Mr Pike drove his electric wheelchair like a racing driver, and I had to jog to keep up.

The manager of the home was a smiley young woman with pink hair, and she took us to the room where I'd be performing. The walls were yellow, and it smelled of toast and the kind of lemony cleaning fluid that Mum uses in the bathroom.

A bearded old man had been alone in the room, in a big, brown armchair, watching a quiz show on the telly, and he wasn't too happy about having it turned off, but he stayed for my show, probably only because leaving seemed like too much effort. Before long, four other people had joined him, two men in wheelchairs, a woman with a walking frame, and one with a walking stick and a large hearing aid.

After the pink-haired lady introduced me, there was

a bit of applause, although most of it was from Mr Pike. And then I stood there in front of them, frozen, before saying the stupidest, lamest, most idiotic first line ever.

'Hi. I'm Magic,' I said, 'and I'm going to do some Holly for you.' Then I closed my eyes and felt my skin get really hot. 'I mean,' I said, mortified, 'the other way around.'

A card fell to the floor during the first trick and the old lady with the hearing aid said, in a very loud voice, 'I think you dropped something, dear!'

For the rope trick, my hands were so shaky that the rope was jiggling around like a live snake.

The man who'd been watching TV dozed off during the next trick, which would have been okay – one less person to watch the unfolding disaster – except that he was a snorer, and not a gentle snorer either. He sounded like one of those big drills that make holes in the road. Everyone was staring at him, until the old woman beside him – the hearing-aid lady – poked him with her walking stick to wake him up.

My last trick was pulling a toy rabbit out of an 'empty' hat, but I yanked the rabbit too hard and swung it around by its ears. There were gasps – and not gasps of wonder either, but people gasping because for a moment they thought that it might be a real rabbit and that I, Holly Chambers, was some kind of evil bunny-torturer.

There was a bit of applause at the end, but most of it seemed to be from Mr Pike again. The others were probably only clapping because they were glad that it was over.

So, I hadn't actually killed any members of the audience – just sent one of them to sleep – but, otherwise, it could hardly have been any worse.

Then the hearing-aid lady came up to me and said loudly, 'Thank you, dear – you really brightened up my morning!'

I smiled back, but I could tell that she was just being kind.

Mr Pike asked me if I'd like a drink of water, but I just wanted to leave. He got the hint, and we set off on the short journey home. More slowly this time. I wasn't in the mood for talking. It felt like I was leaving the scene of a crime.

When I got home I was in a completely terrible mood and, to make things worse, there was a welcoming committee at the front door: Mum – carrying Ernest – with Oates at her feet.

'How did it go?' she asked. I gave her a look. 'Oh,' she said. 'That well, eh?'

I brushed past her, stomped to my room, threw my stupid bag of stupid tricks onto the floor, and threw myself onto the bed.

Mostly I was furious with Mum: for not letting me have any real adventures, for always getting in the way, and for telling Mr Pike that I'd do the show without even asking me.

But I was mad at myself too: for getting so completely nervous. If I'd been that nervous performing in front of just a few random oldies, imagine how terrible I'd be in front of a crowd of hundreds on Friday night – people I knew. I was out of breath just thinking about it.

And, finally, I was angry with Dad. He was in the middle of nowhere, hanging out with reindeer, so I couldn't tell him about the old folk's home disaster or ask him for help with clue number seven. And that was another thing – I was also angry with him for making up such a stupid, impossible clue. *Rex marks the spot –* what on Earth did it mean?

There was a knock on my bedroom door.

'Go away,' I said, but everyone came in anyway. Mum, with her usual concerned look, Ernest, with his stupid dinosaur, and Oates, with his huge flappy tongue lolling stupidly about. 'I want to be alone,' I said – to Mum, mostly. Oates licked me, as if that might help. It didn't. 'I'm giving up on the stupid Dadventure,' I announced. 'And I'm not doing that stupid talent show, either.'

Mum's reaction wasn't at all what I'd expected. She just shrugged, and said, 'If that's what you want, Holly – it's your choice. Though you'll need to tell Mrs Stanley about the talent show.'

I nodded. It would be awkward – my name was on all the posters – and I'd feel like I was letting Mrs Stanley down, but it had to be done.

And then Mum said, 'Look, I know it's probably not a good time, but would you mind having Ernest for a few minutes while I fix the leaky tap in the kitchen?'

I groaned.

Mum went to fix the tap, Oates went along to get in the way, as usual, and Ernest stayed with me – babbling and giggling and swinging his arms around. Even by his standards, he was in a really excitable mood.

I turned my back on him – just for a moment, to reach for a few of the penguin teddies on my bed for him to play with. The next thing I knew, something whacked me on the back of the head.

'Ow!' I said, spinning round.

It was the toy dinosaur. Ernest had hurled it at me and was now looking very anxious, like I might go mad at him. But I didn't. I rubbed my head, and then I actually smiled. Because it wasn't only a prehistoric toy animal that had hit me. It was also the answer to Dad's clue.

'Well, you've certainly brightened up,' Mum said when she came back into my room. 'I'll have to leave Ernest with you more often. I've fixed the tap.'

'And we've solved the clue,' I said.

'We?'

'Ernest helped.'

'Hang on – you wouldn't be talking about that "stupid Dadventure", would you?'

I pulled a face. 'I meant what I said about the talent show though, Mum. I'm not doing it. No way. I can't face it.'

'Fair enough,' she said. 'So – the clue?'

'Rex marks the spot,' I said, pointing at the dinosaur that Ernest was gripping. 'There's a T. rex skeleton at the museum.'

10 Timmy

Once we were at the museum, Mum had promised to let me search for the clue by myself. She had Ernest in his pushchair and, after having a chat to this younger woman who worked at the museum – they seemed to know each other – Mum turned to me and said, 'I'm taking Ernest to the café. Come and join us when your mission's accomplished.'

I watched Mum and Ernest go.

'A mission?' asked the museum woman. She had a ponytail and a nice smile and her name badge said Lauren. 'That sounds intriguing.'

I told her about my dad and the treasure hunt and

'Rex marks the spot'.

'Brilliant,' she said, and pointed to a room. 'Timmy's in there – he's pretty hard to miss.'

'Timmy?'

'That's what we call the T. rex. Happy hunting!'

Timmy, it turned out, was impossible to miss. He was huge, and not even his name stopped him from being terrifying. But where was the clue?

The panel in front of him gave lots of information about T. rexes, but I wasn't so interested in what was *on* it. I remembered where Dad had hidden the clue at the duck pond, and so I crouched and looked underneath the panel. Sure enough, there was the clue, folded up and Blu-tacked. I pulled it off, grinning.

Lauren had walked over to me.

'Sorry,' she said. 'I just couldn't resist. I adore treasure hunts.'

I waved the clue triumphantly in the air.

'No wonder you're so good at finding things,' she said, 'coming from your family.'

'Actually,' I said, 'for an explorer, Dad's really terrible at finding stuff. When he's home, he spends about ten minutes every day looking for his wallet or the TV remote or his car keys. One time he spent half an hour trying to find his shoes!'

She laughed, but said, 'I wasn't actually talking about your dad.'

'Huh?'

'I was talking about your mum.'

I must have looked completely baffled, because she

added, 'Come with me. Let's go on a hunt for some *real* treasure.'

She led me to a room with a large sign saying 'Maya'. There were pictures on the walls and big glass display cabinets with colourful vases or old tools inside. Lauren took me over to a smaller display case and pointed at some tiny green statues of funny-looking people – not much bigger than a finger.

'Jade figurines,' she said. 'Aren't they incredible? A thousand years old, from Guatemala. Such craftsmanship. Such character in their little faces.'

I nodded. They did look brilliant – she was right – but I still had no idea why she was showing them to me.

Then she said, 'It was your mum who found them.'

'Mum?'

I knew that Mum was good at finding things. She'd been the one who'd discovered Dad's missing shoes that time (Oates had hidden them in the garden). Only last week she'd found a pencil, a coin and an old sweet down the back of the sofa. But priceless jade statues?

'She was working with a team from the university,' said Lauren, 'But it was your mum who pinpointed the site. Your mum who helped to dig them up. And your mum who got the Guatemalans to agree to loan them to us for everyone here to see.'

It still didn't make any sense. I mean, I knew that Mum worked part-time at the university – or at least she had until Ernest was born. I knew that she liked old things (and I'm not just talking about Dad – there were lots of books about ancient civilisations on the shelves at home). So I knew her job had something to do with history. But – digging up ancient treasure in a country I'd never even heard of?

What was it with grown-ups? If a kid in my class scores a goal or wins a competition or meets someone from off the telly (or, in Harrison Duffy's case, unearths a particularly good-sized bogey), everyone knows all about it in five seconds flat. But Mr Pike didn't tell me that he'd been a magician, and now my own mum had dug up actual treasure and never even said a word.

'Did you find it?' Mum asked. She'd almost finished her cup of tea and Ernest had smeared most of a fudge brownie on his face. I sat down at their table and showed her the still-folded-up clue. 'Great,' she said. 'Well done!'

=JADE=
FIGURINES

'And I found something else, too.'

'Oh?'

I showed her a leaflet about the jade figurines – I'd taken it for my adventure box.

Mum looked a bit sheepish.

'Right.'

'You didn't tell me you were a treasure hunter,' I said.

'Ha! You make me sound like a pirate!' I felt my face go hot but Mum was smiling. 'I'm an archaeologist, Holly.

A very, very small part of my work is actually digging things up.'

'It still must have been exciting though.'

'Sometimes,' she said.

'And then you had me, and you stopped having adventures.'

'No,' she said. 'I just have different ones now.'

'Toilet-cleaning adventures?' I said, and then looked at Ernest. 'Bottom-wiping adventures?'

This made her snort with laughter, but I wasn't laughing – I just couldn't believe that she'd given it all up, swapped a life of excitement for being a normal, everyday mum.

'Having you, and having Ernest,' she said, 'has been my biggest adventure yet. It's not always glamorous, I will admit. But neither is archaeology, to be honest. It's mostly reading and doing research and filling out tons of boring forms.'

'Dad still gets to have actual adventures around the world,' I said, shaking my head, 'but you have to stay home with us.'

'Dad's job,' she said, 'isn't always breathtakingly

exciting either, you know. A lot of it is him sitting alone in a room, writing the same thing twenty different ways, trying to work out which one is the best.

'Also,' she added, 'I don't *have* to stay at home, Holly. I *choose* to. And in a year or two, in fact, we're planning to swap.'

My eyes widened.

'You mean – you travel, and Dad takes me to school all the time?'

'Maybe. Would you like that?'

'No! Dad's terrible at packed lunches.'

'We've got time to teach him,' Mum said. 'Anyway – we came to the museum for *your* adventure, didn't we? Not to talk about mine.'

I sighed.

'What?' she said.

'It doesn't feel like my adventure, Mum. You've helped with pretty much every task so far.'

'Rubbish.'

'You kept an eye on me climbing the tree, followed me to the duck pond, worked out the photo clue. And you drove me here!'

She sighed, then shrugged.

'*My* most important task,' she said, 'is to keep you kids safe.'

'But you were a real daredevil when you were a kid.'

'I wouldn't say that.'

'I've seen the photos – in the album in the loft.'

She blushed. 'Maybe I was – a bit.'

'And you survived.'

'I suppose I must have.'

'And, in that book I'm reading, the one I got from Mr Pike, Tom Sawyer is having a brilliant adventure, with hardly any grown-ups to bother him. Him and Huck Finn are basically running wild. So,' I said, passionately, 'let me have an adventure too, Mum.'

She sipped on her tea, but didn't take her eyes off mine. Her mind was working, I could tell.

When she put her cup down, she had a very serious expression.

'Did you read the clue yet?' she asked, nodding at the folded-up piece of paper in my hand. I shook my head. She swallowed. 'Whatever the next three tasks are,' she said, 'you can do them by yourself. I won't help, or interfere – unless you want me to.'

'Serious?'

'I promise.'

I leaned over and hugged her.

And then I unfolded the clue.

11 Harold's Peak

Task 8:
Stay calm. Be brave. Don't freak.
Look on top of Harold's Peak.

The next morning, Ernest was playing with a ball on our front lawn, Oates was sniffing around and watering the flowers, as usual, and me and Mum stood facing each other on our front path. I was wearing my birthday present walking boots, a pair of jeans, a top, and a backpack. Mum was looking really pale: I'd never seen her so worried.

Harold's Peak is the name of the highest point in our town. It isn't a huge mountain or anything – it's just a medium-sized hill with a gravel car park at the bottom and a dirt path weaving its way up through loads of trees to the top. I'd climbed it before – with Mum, Dad and Oates, before Ernest was born. It had been really tiring. It had taken more than half an hour from the bottom to the top, and Dad had given me a piggyback some of the way – but I had only been six or seven then. I'm ten now, so it would be a different story. My legs are longer these days for a start.

But Mum was looking incredibly anxious.

'You've got water?' she said.

I patted my backpack and said, 'Check.'

'And you've got my phone?'

I tapped my jeans pocket.

'Check.'

'Whistle?'

'Check. Torch, check. Penknife, check. Band-Aids, check. Banana, check. Brain, check.'

'*Funny*.'

'You aren't going to follow me again are you, Mum?'

'No.'

'And you haven't got a network of neighbourhood spies to watch over me at different places along the route, have you?'

'No . . .' she said. 'Though I'm kicking myself for not thinking of that.' Then she made sure that she had my complete attention. 'If you're not back here in two hours, I'm calling the police . . .'

I sighed.

'. . . and the fire brigade and an ambulance and the army.'

'I get it, Mum.'

'And all the king's horses, and at least most of the king's men.'

'Ha,' I said, but I knew from the look on her face that she was only half joking.

'And call me if there's any trouble – however small.'

'Yep,' I said, but I was determined that I wouldn't call – it would feel like cheating somehow. Like I wasn't doing it on my own.

Then she stepped forward and gave me a hug. A real bone-cruncher.

'Be. Careful,' she said.

When I reached the Pontings' house, I looked back over my shoulder to make sure that Mum wasn't following me. She wasn't, but she was still out on the path watching me. She waved: a little one. It was hard to tell, but it looked like she might have been crying. I'd only ever seen Mum cry at movies before – never at something real – and it made me feel a bit wobbly.

And then I got even wobblier when I saw Emily Fellows sitting on the front step of her house with Jade Skinner next to her. They were both doing something on their phones, and I hoped they wouldn't notice me, but Emily looked up for a moment, spotted me, nudged Jade, and then they both stood up and walked over to the fence.

'Where are you going?' Emily asked.

'Harold's Peak,' I said.

They exchanged a look.

'*Why?*' she said. I shrugged. They both giggled.

I guess it must have seemed pretty weird: someone just deciding to walk up a hill by themselves. But if I'd told them about the Dadventure, that would have seemed even weirder – and besides, I didn't want them knowing about all that.

'Well, have fun,' said Emily – then more giggles and whispering.

With my mum's tears and Emily's teasing I felt like turning back and curling up in my room. But I kept going, past Mr Pike's house and around the corner. And, before long I'd forgotten about everything – Emily, Mum, Dad. Everything.

The streets were quiet and Sunday-ish – there were hardly any cars around. You could actually hear birds in the trees. Mum had checked the weather on her phone before giving it to me: cloudy, no rain. Perfect walking weather.

It felt like a real adventure.

It felt brilliant. I felt free.

When I got to the empty car park though, and stared at the dirt track swerving up the hill in front of me, that feeling of freedom and confidence and excitement – it just kind of slipped away.

And I might have been imagining it, but the clouds seemed suddenly darker, more threatening, and the hill looked steeper than I remembered too. The path was littered with stones and snaked with branches and tree roots – lots of things that you could trip on. I felt incredibly lonely. And my feet were starting to hurt – my new shoes were rubbing at the heels with every step. But I took a deep breath and started climbing.

It wasn't long, though, before my heels were so sore that I had to hobble and, not long after that, I couldn't take a step without wincing. So I sat on a tree stump. I was out of breath, and upset, and really annoyed with myself. Very slowly, I took off my boots and peeled off my socks.

I gasped. It really stung! I had to bite my lip to stop myself from crying. On both heels were red circles the size of small coins. I took the Band-Aids out of my backpack and carefully stuck them on. Then back on with my socks and shoes. I was grimacing from the pain, and muttering to myself: it was all my fault. I should have broken the new shoes in. Walked around the garden in them. I should have worn two pairs of socks.

I took a couple of steps – it wasn't quite as painful as before, but it was still really uncomfortable.

I stopped. Tried to think.

The sensible thing, I realised, would be to call Mum. Get her to bring the car and meet me in the car park. It wouldn't be giving up, I told myself – I had a good excuse for stopping. And besides, I could come back in a few days when my feet felt better, in a comfortable old pair of trainers, and I'd still have enough time to complete the Dadventure.

I took the phone out of my pocket.

It was the screensaver that stopped me – a photo of the family. All of us were smiling, even Ernest, but I looked into Dad's eyes. Even when he smiled, he had this determined look – *he* wouldn't be giving up now, at the first sign of trouble. No way. He'd get to the top. So I put the phone back in my pocket, tried to ignore the pain, and kept on climbing.

Half an hour later – but the blisters made it feel much, much longer – I scrambled the last few metres over the loose ground and reached the top of the hill. My whole body ached – not just my feet. I was wheezing, my calves were tight, my heels agony. I didn't feel proud, just tired, angry at myself for getting blisters, and anxious to find the clue. I shrugged off my backpack, unzipped it, pulled out the water bottle, swigged, and felt the water slide down my throat and into my tummy.

The top of the hill was a flattish area of dirt, no bigger than our back garden. There were a few clumps of grass and a few tiny purple flowers. I picked one and put it in my backpack to put into my adventure-kit-turned-memory-box, later. There was no bench or lookout platform up here or anything like that, but there was a thick tree trunk that had been struck by lightning long ago – it was scorched and lying flat to the ground. When I'd come here with Mum and Dad, we'd sat on that tree trunk, eaten our sandwiches and looked out at the view. But today there was no time for that. I had to find the clue. Where had Dad hidden it?

The tree trunk was the only real hiding place. I walked around it and peered into every hole or crack I could find – any places where Dad could have stuffed a small piece of paper.

At the far end of the trunk there was a crack, not quite wide enough to fit a finger inside, but with enough room for a clue. I got on my knees and squinted into it. There was definitely something in there. I took the penknife out of my backpack, wiggled it inside the crack and dragged the thing out.

At first it seemed like just a piece of litter – some clear plastic, torn from a supermarket bag. But when I looked more closely, I saw it was actually a tiny parcel, sticky-taped! I tore it open. Inside was a slip of paper. I unfolded it and read the message.

Task 9:
Well done, Holly! How's the view?
You're nearly finished! The 9th clue:
Using the map and the key that you've got,
Find a buried chest - X marks the spot!

I couldn't stop grinning. I forgot, for a moment, about the blisters.

Even more than finding the clue, I just loved the idea of Dad coming here by himself to hide it. While I was at school, Dad would have been planting clues at the museum or the duck pond, or visiting Mr Pike's house or Gary's Chinese takeaway. And all of it for me.

I just couldn't wait to get home and tell Mum all about my epic adventure - climbing the hill and finding the clue.

And then there was suddenly another reason to get down the hill quickly - a surprise rumble of thunder, like a distant drum roll on one of those big drums they have in orchestras. I looked up at the sky. The clouds were definitely darker – grey-black. The breeze was picking up. A storm was coming, and coming soon, whatever Mum's phone had said.

I shoved the penknife and the clue into my backpack, zipped it up, slung it on and started back down the hill. It was quicker going downhill – much quicker, but more dangerous too.

I'd almost got used to the blisters now, though I'd had to develop a shuffly way of walking to lessen the pain.

Halfway down, I felt the first drops of rain. Big fat cold ones. Then a flash of lightning – it lit up the gloom for a moment. A crack of thunder made me jump. It wasn't overhead – not quite, but getting louder, closer. Scarier. I wanted to be home. The rain had got heavy very quickly, making the path slippy and soaking me. My hair was pasted to my head, my top and jeans stuck to my body. I kept on moving – shuffling and skidding, blinking water out of my eyes.

And then I tripped – a tree root across the path. I didn't see it. For a second I was flying – my elbows and knees were flailing. Then a second later the ground

whacked me, exploded the breath out of me.

I yelped, but it was drowned out by the noise of rain on leaves. I stayed there sprawled on my tummy, trying to get my breath back.

My palms stung where they'd slapped the ground. They felt like they were on fire. I moved my wrists slowly, first the right and then the left: they seemed okay though – nothing broken. I pushed off the ground and slowly got to my feet.

Not okay.

My left ankle. I'd rolled over on it in the fall, and even standing was horribly painful. I whimpered, gritted my teeth and tried to take a half-step forward, but I couldn't put any pressure on it.

I leaned against a tree and pulled the phone out of my wet pocket to call Mum. I had no choice now. Yes, it would mean that I'd failed. But I needed help. My ankle was screaming in pain – either badly twisted or broken. And I was right in the middle of a thunderstorm.

I squinted at the phone. Rain streamed down it. I wiped it on my jeans. But the screen was blank.

I pressed the button on the top and then the one on the side. Then I pressed them both together.

Nothing.

This was bad. Very bad.

I was alone. Completely. Not even the photo of my family on the screensaver was there to comfort me any more.

My ankle – broken, or at least too painful to walk on. The phone – definitely broken. It was still raining buckets. Thunder. Lightning. Dad had told me not to shelter under a tree when lightning was about. But I was surrounded by trees now, and leaning against one for balance – it was impossible to escape them here.

I had two choices – that was clear. I could wait here, cold, wet, alone, risking lightning bolts, and hope that Mum called 999. Or I could try to make it home myself.

I knew that I had to try at least.

I looked around in the hard rain. On the ground, not far from me, was a branch – straight-ish, and the right length for a walking stick. I bent awkwardly, picked it up and leaned on it to test it – it was solid – and started hobbling. But straight away I realised that it would take me forever to get down the hill like that. So I tried a new tactic: hopping.

Hop. Hop. Hop – using the branch to steady me on the slippy surface. Hop. Hop. Rest.

More lightning, like the flash from a giant camera. A clap of thunder that went right through me.

Hop. Hop. Hop. I had to get to the bottom.

Hop. Hop. Rest. I was cold. Soaked. Out of breath. But I had to get home.

Hop. Hop. Hop. I slipped. Yelped. Got straight back up.

Hop. Hop. Hop.

12 Buried Treasure

Hop. Hop. Rest. I blinked the rain from my eyes. It was hard to see more than a few metres in front of me. I wasn't even sure that I was still on the path. What if I was lost?

And then, through the trees, through the heavy rain, I saw lights. *I must be close to the bottom*, I thought. A torch? No – car headlights. Pointing towards me – dazzling me, highlighting the rain. I squinted. Kept hopping. The car wasn't moving, but someone had got out of the driver's door and was coming this way. I could see a shape – a person. I tensed up, gripped the stick tighter.

And then I saw:

It was *Mum*. My shoulders relaxed – my whole body.
I'd never been so relieved to see someone.

She was jogging towards me, already soaked.

I was expecting her to be mad, to tell me off, but
instead she hugged me. I dropped the stick.

'Why didn't you answer my calls?' she said, but her tone was relieved, not angry. 'I was *this* far from calling the police.'

'The phone's not working.'

'You're drenched,' she said. 'And – limping?'

'My ankle. I tripped. That must be when the phone broke.'

'Let's get you into the dry,' Mum said. She supported me as I hopped towards the car, then she opened the passenger door and told me to wait. She fetched Oates's towel from the boot, wrapped me in it and helped me into the passenger seat. We were both dripping wet. She closed my door and got into the driver's seat.

Ernest was in his car seat in the back, gurgling with pleasure as the rain drummed noisily on the roof.

'I was worried the storm might freak him out,' Mum said – shouted really, above the din of the rain. 'But he's never had so much fun. Turns out he loves the thunder – I'm afraid we might have another adventurer on our hands!'

She slid my seat back so I could stretch my left leg out. Then she reached down and examined the ankle.

She'd done a first-aid course once apparently, although she must have missed the bit where they're taught how to be gentle. She prodded my ankle.

'Ow!' I said. And then, 'Ouch, Mum!'

'It's swollen,' she said. 'Sprained, I think – not broken. If it was broken, you'd be screaming your head off right now.' And then she started up the engine. The windscreen wipers came on – full speed – but you could hardly hear them over the drumming of the rain on the roof.

Mum drove carefully out of the car park. 'How are you otherwise?' she asked.

I wasn't sure. I was relieved, partly. In pain too – my ankle throbbing. I was cold. Wet. But mostly I had this overwhelming feeling of disappointment. That was it – I was bitterly disappointed. With myself – my first real adventure, and I'd needed rescuing. By my mum. And it wasn't just me that I'd let down. It was Dad too.

'Tell me what happened,' Mum said kindly.

I told her – about the blisters, about getting to the top, finding the clue, the rain, tripping over, everything. And then I said, 'Are you angry?' though I could hardly bring myself to hear the answer.

'Angry?' she said. 'With you?' She turned to glance at me. I nodded. 'Absolutely *not*, Holly. Not in the slightest. I'm angry with Dad – a bit. I'm mostly mad at myself, for relying on a weather forecast from a mobile phone.'

'What about your phone, Mum?'

'I needed a new one, anyway,' she said. 'Look – I don't give two hoots about my phone – you're safe, Holly. That's the only thing that matters right now.'

My head hung forward. I sighed.

'What is it, Sausage?' Mum said.

'Dad's a famous explorer,' I said.

'Travel writer,' she corrected.

'And *you* dug up actual treasure, Mum. But I can't even climb a hill without getting into trouble!'

'Are you kidding me?' she said, but her tone was amused, not angry. 'You climbed down a steep hill. Alone. In a thunderstorm. On one leg. Aged *ten*. Holly – I could not *be* more proud.'

I was suddenly fuzzy with happiness.

'And another thing,' she added. 'If your ankle's really sore . . .'

'It *is*. It really is.'

'Then you should rest it. Perhaps you should even pull out of the talent show.'

A huge grin spread over my face. She was right – I wouldn't have to perform now, and Mrs Stanley would understand. It was perfect. Perfect. I felt this incredible lightness – a wave of relief. A sore ankle seemed a very small price to pay for completing the task *and* avoiding the humiliation on Friday.

When Dad called that evening, I was lying on the sofa with my left foot resting on a cushion and a bag of frozen sweetcorn balanced on my ankle. Mum answered the phone and put Dad on speaker.

'And how's my favourite non-reindeer family?' he asked.

'Ernest is sleeping, finally,' Mum said with a sigh. 'I'm completely exhausted. And your daughter, while completing your latest hare-brained task, has got blisters on her feet the size of dinner plates –' which was a slight exaggeration – 'and she's really hurt her ankle.' Which was not.

'I'm okay, Dad!' I said. My ankle was still really sore

and the blisters stung, but I was happy – I'd had an actual adventure and lived to tell the tale. But Dad was quiet for a moment.

'I'm sorry, Princess. What happened?'

'I got the blisters going up Harold's Peak. And twisted my ankle on the way down. But I found the clue.'

'You've finished task eight already? That's incredible!'

I told him all about tasks five, six, seven and – especially – eight.

'You're some kind of daredevil, all right,' said Dad.

'A daredevil who can hardly walk,' said Mum. She looked like she was about to go on a bit of a rant, and so I quickly changed the subject: I'd picked up this talent from Dad of course, the king of subject-changing.

'How's *your* adventure going?' I asked him.

'Not nearly as exciting as yours, by the sound of it. Reindeers,' he said, 'really, really stink.' I laughed. 'I mean it,' he said. 'Imagine Brussels sprouts, boiled in a sweaty sock, and smothered in runny cheese.'

'That sounds like Mum's cooking,' I quipped.

'Hey,' said Mum.

'Tomorrow,' Dad continued, 'I'm riding with huskies, and I hear that they pong a fair bit too – like Oates, times ten.'

'Yuck.'

Dad giggled and then said, 'I'm really sorry about your ankle, Lolly.'

'It's okay, Dad. It was really worth it!'

'I'm super-proud of you – and only two tasks to go.'

That reminded me.

'You said in the clue that I've already got the key and the map.'

'Correct.'

'The key's the one in the adventure kit, right?'

'It might be,' he said.

'But where's the map, Dad?'

He hesitated.

'You'll have to work that one out yourself, I'm afraid,' he said. And no amount of pestering would change his mind.

After we'd hung up, I hopped to my room and looked through the shoebox, which was now less of an adventure kit and more of a treasure chest. The tiny purple flower from Harold's Peak – like me a bit battered, but still remarkably in one piece – was now in with all the other mementoes. I wondered if I'd somehow missed a folded-up map that Dad had tucked in to the box – but I hadn't. The key was in there, of course. I took it out and slipped it into my pocket, hopped back down the stairs – holding onto the banister – and then sagged back onto the sofa. I was so close, but I wouldn't be able to finish the Dadventure without that map, and Dad wasn't going to give me any more clues.

Incredibly, it was Oates who pointed me in the right direction. Not on purpose – he was much too daft for that. But he suddenly started barking and jumping up – it was his usual nemesis, a fly, hovering above the shelf where my birthday cards were still on display. That's when I noticed it. Not the fly, but my dad's birthday card. It had a map – of course! A really silly one, but it was still a map, and it did have an 'X' on it.

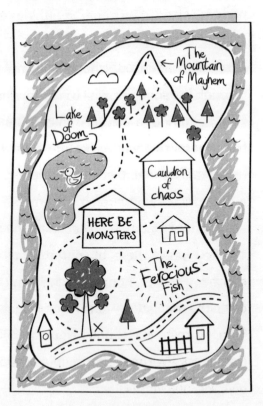

So I jumped up, calmed Oates down, and hopped over to the shelf. I picked up the card and brought it back to the sofa to study it.

Dad's map was of an island, but there were no islands near here, and the place names were much too silly to be real. Plus, considering the trouble I'd just had on a medium-sized hill, it was probably a good idea to stay well away from The Mountain of Mayhem.

Not to mention The Lake of Doom.

Wait – what was that on the lake? Was it – a tiny duck?

'Ha!' I said.

Mum had been in the kitchen, making hot chocolates for us both, but she poked her head back in.

'What?' she said.

I waved the card at her.

'It's our town!' I said excitedly. 'The Lake of Doom is the duck pond, and The Mountain of Mayhem must be Harold's Peak.' I was speaking really quickly, the words tumbling out. 'Which makes The Cauldron of Chaos the Chinese restaurant, and "Here Be Monsters" is in the right place for the museum, look – the "monsters" must be the dinosaurs.'

Then I frowned.

'What about The Ferocious Fish though? None of the tasks have had any fish in them. And, if the duck pond's *there*, and Wok Around the Clock is *here*, then "The Ferocious Fish" must be really nearby.'

Now it was Mum's turn to laugh.

'What?' I said.

'Mr Pike! A pike's a fish, isn't it? A pretty ferocious one too!'

'And that tree,' I said, breathlessly, 'must be Lofty!' I was giddy with excitement. 'So the next clue must be buried in our garden!' I jumped up – I remembered to land on my good foot. 'Let's go dig it up!'

'Steady on,' said Mum. 'It's pretty late, love, and it's a school day tomorrow. And you really do need to rest that ankle.'

I sighed – a really long one. But then Mum smiled and winked.

'If you *really* want to,' she said, 'you can do it now.'

I smiled back at her.

'Can you come too?' I asked.

'You want me to help?' she said in disbelief.

'Yes, please. Your treasure-hunting experience might come in handy. Also, it will be good to have someone to lean on.'

Mum grinned.

I hopped out to the garden. Oates followed me and then, a minute later, Mum came outside too, with her hands full: I'd asked her to get the torch from my backpack, the metal detector from the shed and one of those tiny spade things that archaeologists use.

I knew exactly where to look – the veggie patch. It had to be. Any other place, and you'd be able to tell where Dad had dug the ground up.

It's not easy using a metal detector while hopping about, but I used Mum for balance and she shone a torch at the ground. We were like a team. A team of archaeologists.

Bleep!

I whooped, crouched awkwardly, and Mum handed me the tiny spade.

'Is this the same tool that you uncovered the jade statues with?' I asked.

'It's called a trowel,' she said. 'And yes, it is, actually.'

I grinned and dug, excitedly. And discovered . . . an old bottle top. Mum helped me back to my feet and I hopped around some more, sweeping the detector over the dirt. Oates was completely getting in the way of course. To him, this was some kind of brilliant new game. The next bleep was, in fact, his collar.

Seconds later, another bleep. I dug, deeper this time, until Oates, barking, nudged me aside and used his back paws to dig – dirt went flying everywhere. Mum found this hilarious – she was hooting with laughter and the torch was jiggling around in her hand. But then a paw struck metal – thunk.

'Good boy!' I said, ruffling his fur. I gently shoved him aside, cleared the dirt and, in the torchlight, saw a small black tin like a moneybox.

'The treasure chest!' I said.

I lifted it out, took the key from my pocket and put it in the keyhole. It fitted! When I turned the key, the lid sprang open. I'd hoped that the box would be crammed with shiny stuff, like a real treasure chest. It wasn't.

Inside was a single piece of paper. It said:

Task 10:
You're nearly done!
Break a leg and have some fun!

My mouth dropped open. *Break a leg?*

My dad must have completely lost his mind. I could hardly walk as it was.

Mum was shaking her head and smiling.

'What does he mean – *break a leg*?' I asked her.

'It's what performers say to each other before they go on stage,' she explained. 'It's just a daft way of saying "good luck".'

But I still didn't understand.

'Your final task,' she said, 'must be your performance. At the talent show.'

I closed my eyes, suddenly feeling sick.

13 Hollidini

'What *have* you done to that leg of yours?' asked Mr Pike, after I'd limped down his hall and flopped into my usual chair. He chuckled. 'You don't need to borrow this, do you?' he said, tapping the side of his wheelchair.

I smiled and shook my head, and then I told him all about tasks seven, eight and nine, and finally about the fast-approaching nightmare of task ten this coming Friday.

'I've got to do it,' I told him grimly, 'even though my ankle's still sore – and just *thinking* about being on stage in front of all those people makes me want to throw up. But I can't give up, can I? Not when I'm this close to the end.' Mr Pike nodded. 'And – I was wondering if you could give me some help,' I said. 'So I don't have another complete disaster like the one at the old people's home. That would be horrible.'

'It wasn't a *complete* disaster,' he said. I gave him a look. 'A *slight* disaster, I'll grant you that. But not a complete one.' He smiled. 'You just got really nervous, that's all. It happens.'

'But if I get that nervous in front of some random old folks,' I said, 'just think how I'm going to be on Friday, in front of hundreds of people – and people that I actually know.'

'Have you ever noticed,' he said, leaning forward, 'how the feeling of being nervous is almost exactly the same as the feeling of excitement? Think about it: your tummy feels all light. It's hard to keep still. Your brain can't think of anything else.' I nodded – it was true. 'So, on Friday, instead of thinking about how incredibly nervous you are, just tell yourself instead that you're really, really *excited*. It sounds simple, I know, but I promise you that it helps. Okay?'

'I'll try.'

'Also,' he continued, 'you need an onstage persona.

Do you know what that is?'

'Not really.'

'When I stepped on stage,' he said, 'I ceased to be Reg Pike. I was The Amazing Mysterio. I might have looked like the same man, but I felt entirely different – more confident, more dashing. And Janet was normally a rather shy person but onstage, wearing a sparkly dress

and make-up, she had the glamour of a movie star. And then, after each show, we would change out of our stage clothes, drive home and slip back into our old selves – watch a bit of television, play a game of cribbage, have a cup of tea.'

'So I need a persona,' I said.

'Exactly.'

'But what if I haven't got one?'

'You do,' he said. 'Practically everyone's got several. For instance, think of how you are when you're at home with your parents, and then think about how you behave when you're at school. I'll bet that you're not exactly the same Holly in both of those places, are you?'

'No,' I said. He was completely right, of course. At school I was usually quiet these days – like I was hiding who I really was so that people would leave me alone. Except that it wasn't really working: it wasn't making me happy, and those girls kept on teasing me anyway.

'I have another persona too,' said Mr Pike. 'Pike the Spike.' He was smiling pleasantly, but it was really shocking to hear him say the name. 'The story goes that I'm a knife-wielding maniac who pounces on every ball that comes into my garden and slashes it to pieces. Have you heard it?'

I squirmed and blushed – then I nodded guiltily.

'Well, it's complete nonsense,' he said. 'The screechy girl from next door was playing in the garden one day, with some equally noisy friends. Their ball sailed over the fence – and not for the first time either, I might add. But on this occasion it landed smack bang in the middle of the flower bed. Janet's flower bed.'

We both looked out at it now, through the window.

'She'd died the year before, and that garden was her thing, Holly. Her passion. She was always out there, all seasons, planting, pruning, or just pottering around. So when that ball came over and crushed some of her daffodils – snapped the stems – I'm afraid to say that I sort of snapped too. I went out to the garden, shook my fist at those kids and shouted that I would burst the next ball that came over. Then I tossed their ball back and went inside.

'So, the truth is that I haven't stabbed so much as *one* ball. Not ever. And nor do I have any intention of doing so. But the name seems to have stuck, Holly, and

157

it's not an entirely terrible thing, between you and me. Put it this way – no balls have landed in my garden since. Not a single one. Now, what was I talking about?'

'Personas,' I said.

'Ah, yes. You just need an "On-stage Holly". A "Magic Holly" – that's all. Now, tell me – what are you planning to wear on Friday night?'

I shrugged.

'Just normal clothes, I guess.'

He shook his head.

'That will never do, Holly. You need to wear something special. Something that says "prepare to be entertained".'

'Well,' I said, blushing, 'Mum bought me a sparkly bow tie for my birthday, but . . .'

'Perfect,' he said. 'Just perfect. And you need a name.' He was quiet for a moment, and then he said, 'The Incredible Holly.'

'After the disaster at the old people's home,' I said, 'I should be calling myself The Completely Terrible Holly.'

'Hollidini!' he said. 'That's it! After the great escapologist, Harry Houdini, who himself was named after the great magician, Robert Houdin. Hollidini,' he repeated, as if the matter had been decided.

'Everyone will just laugh at me,' I said firmly.

'So, don't *tell* anyone. Your name can be a secret thing, if you like – just for you.' He tapped his head. 'It's all about believing in yourself – and not worrying too much about what other people think.'

'Okay,' I said.

'And finally,' he continued, 'you need a showstopper. You've got some decent tricks. You've got some decent skills, when the nerves don't get the better of you. But we need something at the end of your performance – something to make the audience gasp, and then cheer. We need a proper finale, an exclamation mark.'

'But there's only four days before the show,' I said weakly.

'That's true,' he conceded. 'It's not much time to learn something new, is it?'

That's when I had the idea: an idea that was either truly brilliant or completely stupid.

'Do you still have all your old equipment?' I asked. 'From your magic days?'

'Yes,' he said, his face lighting up. 'I couldn't bring myself to get rid of it. Come and look.'

He motored out of the living room and back down the hall. I followed him. There was a door on the left, which he pushed open. I stepped inside.

'Wow!' I said.

I looked around the room in complete wonder, and then looked at Mr Pike. He was grinning at my reaction,

and another thought struck me.

'You told me that you're an ex-magician.'

'I am.'

'But you didn't give any of this stuff away?'

'Too much effort,' he said, but I didn't believe him.

It's like the dolls that I have in my bottom drawer. I've grown out of them now, but I just can't bring myself to give them away yet, because they still mean something to me. Something special.

'When you were showing me that trick last time,' I said, 'you had this kind of twinkle in your eye . . .'

He laughed.

'. . . and now, when you see all your magic things, you've got the same look. It's like magic is a part of you, Mr Pike. And you can't ignore such a big part of your life, can you? You can't lock it away in here, in a box.'

As I was saying this, I knew that it was what *I* was doing at school too – hiding who I really was. I was locking myself away from everyone, hiding my personality. And I realised then that it had to stop.

'Speaking of boxes,' said Mr Pike, his eyes twinkling again, 'take a look at that cabinet over there – I built it myself. Let me show you how it works.'

14   The Show

From the side of the stage, half-hidden by the curtain, I looked out at the audience.

My heart was thumping. I could hardly breathe.

On the stage, Year Six girls were dancing in matching pink-and-purple costumes. The music was loud, and they were pretty good, but I could hardly watch. My tummy felt light, like a balloon.

The school hall was completely packed. I started counting the audience. I got to a hundred, and then I stopped: it wasn't helping. And it wasn't just how many people either, but *which* people. Kids that I knew, teachers, parents. Emily Fellows was there, just waiting for the chance to laugh at me, I was certain of that – and it wouldn't just be her laughing either.

The rock-climbing disaster had taken me weeks to live down. If tonight went badly, the teasing could go on for months – years even.

My mum was on the end of the front row, with Ernest on her lap. Mr Pike was next to them in his electric wheelchair.

There was no sign of Dad. I knew that he wasn't supposed to be back for another week, but I'd had this crazy idea that he'd turn up at the last minute, like in a movie: he would cut his adventure short, and dash back – a last-minute flight, then a taxi from the airport screeching to a halt in the school car park and Dad flinging open the taxi door and sprinting inside, just in time. I looked to see if he was standing at the back of the hall, out of breath. But he wasn't there.

My chest felt tight, and I had to remember to breathe.

I knew from the Dadventure that things which seemed completely terrifying at first – climbing the tree, visiting scary neighbours, eating things that looked like deep-fried worms – often turned out to be nothing to worry about. And if I could survive hobbling down a hill in a thunderstorm, I could surely survive a talent show. I knew all this, and yet none of it calmed me down.

I decided – too late – that I looked completely ridiculous. Mr Pike had somehow talked me into the bow tie, but it looked incredibly stupid. I had a tiny microphone headset attached to my ear, like pop singers have, and that looked really daft too.

I'm excited, I told myself. *Not nervous – excited.* I closed my eyes and said it to myself, over and over. It actually helped – a bit. But I was still shaking. And I still looked stupid.

The song finished. The girls stopped dancing, more or less at the same time, and took a bow, together. I'd been hoping that they would go on forever. I was next, and everyone had been good so far: a piano player from Year Three, two singers, a juggler. Even Harrison Duffy's musical armpit had knocked them dead – in a good way. Mrs Stanley said, after his performance, that it was one of the most interesting renditions of *Twinkle, Twinkle, Little Star* that she'd ever heard.

She was back on stage with the microphone.

'That was Four-Mation!' she boomed. 'Give them another big cheer!'

When the clapping died down, Mrs Stanley said, 'And now, to dazzle you with some tricks . . .'

I gulped. 'Dazzle'. Even more pressure.

'. . . it's the magical Holly Chambers.'

There was a lot of clapping. Mrs Stanley was beckoning me, but I didn't feel like I could move.

I took a deep breath.

And then I walked – still with a bit of a limp – and stopped next to the small table that the stagehands had put front-centre stage. I looked at the table – all my tricks were on there. And then I stared out at the audience. The spotlight was too bright. It made me squint.

The clapping had stopped now, and had been replaced with an uncomfortable silence. There were a few coughs.

I picked up the pack of cards from the table and concentrated on not dropping them.

'An ordinary pack of cards,' I said quietly – too quietly. No one heard me: my microphone wasn't working. Out of the corner of my eye, I could see the sound person – a boy from my class – scrabbling around, plugging things in. He nodded, so I started again.

'An ordinary pack of cards,' I said, louder this time, but now the microphone was turned up too loud, like I was shouting, and there was a horrible squealing noise from the speakers. Lots of laughter. I could pick out the screechy laugh of Emily Fellows. I swallowed, and said, 'Could I have a volunteer, please, to shuffle the pack for me?'

An older kid in the front row put his hand up. I invited him up to the stage and passed him the cards – he shuffled them and went to hand them back.

'A bit more,' I said. 'Really mix them up.'

He did, and then I thanked him, took the cards and, as he sat back down, I looked at the audience.

'And now,' I said, 'I'm going to read your minds.' There was a burst of laughter. It was really nice to make people laugh on purpose – a warm feeling flowed up my back. 'I want you all to concentrate on each card I show you.'

When I got the first one wrong, there was another uncomfortable silence.

I glanced over at Mum and Ernest, but it was Mr Pike, beside them, who caught my eye. He was mouthing something. 'Hollidini.'

I remembered his advice, about my onstage persona: be more confident, more fearless.

I took another deep breath.

'I need you all to concentrate a bit harder, please,' I said to the audience. More laughter – good laughter, which really helped me relax. And I got the next card right, which helped even more. After that I got into a good rhythm. Bang. Bang. Bang. After correctly identifying five cards, it was time for my next trick. I put down the cards and bowed. There was a lot of applause.

The rope trick was a lot less shaky than at the old people's home, and that got a good-sized clap too. So did the rabbit-from-the-hat. There was another big, rolling laugh when they saw that the bunny was a toy. I was actually starting to enjoy myself, but the finale was going to be the hardest bit and I was terrified of getting it wrong.

'For my final trick,' I said, 'I need a volunteer.' I pretended to look around the audience. Lots of kids had their hands up. 'It really needs to be an adult,' I said. 'Because this trick is incredibly dangerous.'

More laughter. It felt brilliant, a warm burst of joy that made my whole body tingle.

Mr Pike's hand was up, just like we'd practised.

'You, sir,' I said. He looked around, as if I might be pointing at someone else. 'Yes, you, sir. Would you please come up here?'

There was a ramp leading to the stage – I'd arranged it with Mrs Stanley earlier. Mr Pike manoeuvred his wheelchair up it and stopped right next to me, facing the audience.

'And what's your name, sir?' I asked him.

'Reg,' he answered, in a loud voice. 'Reg Pike.'

I heard a few gasps. Some kids had realised who it was. I heard whispers – *Pike the Spike*.

'And are you at all squeamish, sir? Do you have any problems, for example, with the sight of blood?'

There was uneasy laughter from the audience. Mr Pike shook his head.

'Good,' I said.

I fetched the cabinet from behind the curtain where it had been waiting.

The cabinet was black and looked like a large upright coffin on small wheels. I pushed it to the centre of the stage beside Mr Pike. Then I opened the door to show everyone that the cabinet was completely empty, and spun it around 360 degrees so that the audience could see it from every angle.

'I am going to get inside this ordinary cabinet,' I announced. 'And then you, sir, on my instructions –' I paused for effect – 'will push a blade right through the side here.'

There were fewer laughs from the grown-ups now, and a lot more gasps from the kids. I could see Emily Fellows looking pale, her mouth wide open – and other kids had that same expression too. When I picked up the silver sword from the table and handed it to Mr Pike I thought some of them were actually going to faint.

'Now – are you able to be trusted with sharp blades, Mr Pike?' I said. He nodded. 'And could you confirm that this blade is indeed solid?'

He flicked it with a finger and it made a loud 'ping'. He nodded again.

Then I stepped inside the cabinet, closed the door behind me, and slid back the small square of wood in front of my face so the audience could see that I hadn't escaped.

'On the count of three, sir, could you please insert that blade into the side of the wardrobe? But FIRST –' the audience was silent – 'please remember that my mum and my little brother are in the audience tonight, and they would really miss me if I wasn't around.'

This got a big laugh from the grown-ups. Not from the kids. The kids looked terrified.

I couldn't see Mr Pike, but I knew what he was doing: he would be gripping the blade, ready to thrust it into the side of the wardrobe.

'One . . .' I said. 'Two . . . Two and a half . . .' – more laughter – 'Three!'

And with a flourish, Mr Pike pushed the blade – hard – into the side of the cabinet.

I squealed.

There were gasps. Not only from the kids. Then, silence.

The blade was real, but the cabinet was a trick one, with mirrors and a false back – it looked to the audience like the sword was going through the middle of the cabinet, and through the middle of me, but the blade had slid safely into the back part.

Mr Pike pulled out the sword – more gasps – and then . . .

I flung the door open, burst out, stepped forward, arms wide, and took a bow.

There was a *huge* round of applause. It sounded like thunder. It bounced off the walls of the hall! There were even some cheers. I looked at Mum – she was whistling, her fingers in her mouth, and then she was cheering too.

I caught her eye and pressed the button on my bow tie – it lit up and spun around. More laughter, more applause.

Mrs Stanley was back on stage, saying, 'The amazing Holly, everyone! She's still in one piece, ladies and gentlemen! Children, please do not try that at home!'

And there was more laughing and clapping and cheering.

I was completely out of breath.

My heart was thumping.

It was brilliant.

15　The Treasure Chest

I'd been wrong about Mr Pike. Twice.

At first, I'd thought he was really scary, and that turned out to be completely wrong. Later, when I knew him a bit, I'd thought he seemed pretty happy to be by himself, at home, with his books and his memories. But that was wrong too.

I realised this on the night of the talent show. I'd seen how happy he was – on stage, but also afterwards, being introduced to people by Mum, chatting with them, smiling. I realised that, when you cut yourself off from people, it's normal to get a bit lonely. It was true for Mr Pike. And it was also true for me.

So, at school on Monday, still buzzing from the

Dadventure and the talent show, I decided to be myself. I put my hand up more in class, ignored the predictable giggles, and talked to more people at break. I did something else unusual too – I invited Asha Chopra to our house. She checked with her mum – who said yes! – and then Asha came over tonight: Wednesday.

We played the chopsticks game at the kitchen table. Asha was completely terrible at it. She couldn't stop laughing, and neither could I. Oates had a brilliant time too, snaffling Asha's peanuts as they tumbled to the floor.

Me, I was pretty deadly with a pair of chopsticks by now. My personal best was fifteen peanuts in thirty seconds.

After we'd eaten the surviving peanuts (and some biscuits that Mum had baked specially, washed down with cold milk), Asha and I went to my room. From under my bed, I pulled out the treasure chest. I was really nervous about showing it to her – what if she thought it was stupid? – but I did it anyway. I talked her through the whole adventure, using the mementoes as props, and she seemed totally enthralled.

When I'd finished, she shook her head in wonder.

'You have a really cool dad,' she said.

I smiled, but shook my head.

'If you'd ever seen him dancing, you wouldn't say that,'
I said. 'He dances like someone who's being attacked by
bees.'

She laughed.

'What a great adventure, though,' she said, and
I nodded.

After Asha's mum picked her up (and invited me to their place next week!), I went back to my room and looked through the treasure chest by myself.

First, I picked up the leaf from Lofty – it seemed like ages ago that I was halfway up the tree, hugging it, scared out of my mind. Then I looked through the programme from the talent show – I'd been thinking about my performance a lot over the last week, replaying it like a favourite movie in my head, and remembering that incredible feeling I'd got when everyone had laughed, or clapped, or cheered. And I wasn't just reliving the performance, but what had happened after too: kids and teachers and parents all congratulating me, telling me how brilliant it was, how much they'd enjoyed themselves.

Dad had told me in his letter that you didn't have to travel to have an adventure, and I hadn't really believed him at the time, but now I saw that he was right.

I looked at the moneybox that I'd dug up in task nine, and at the jade-statue leaflet that I'd brought home from the museum. I'd thought that the Dadventure would be all about me and Dad, but instead I'd learned a whole lot about my mum. And about Mr Pike too. I think Dad had planned it that way. He was saying: you don't have to travel the world to meet interesting people. They could be living in your street. Or even in your house.

And on top of all this, I'd learned a lot about myself: I'd learned that I could still surprise myself. I'd realised just how much I was capable of.

From downstairs, Oates started barking, and this jolted me out of my happy thoughts. Had he spotted a fly? Or had he heard something outside? Yes – seconds later, there was a knock at the door. A quick double-knock: Dad's knock!

I jumped up too – my ankle was pretty much back to normal by now – and I rushed down to the front door and flung it open.

It was him!

Dad had grown a beard and he was bent forward under the weight of his enormous backpack. He was carrying two shopping bags full of presents, one in each hand but, when he saw me, he dropped them, stepped into the hall, scooped me up and hugged me – *squeezed* me, actually – a real bear hug, a bone-cruncher, squishing the breath out of me.

'How's my incredible adventurer?' he said.

'She's finding it hard to breathe,' I wheezed, and so he put me gently down. I grinned.

Mum, holding Ernest, was behind me by now. Dad took my brother, kissed him, hugged him, weighed him, said how much bigger he was, asked him how the piano lessons were going – and then Dad smooched Mum. Oates jumped up at them, barking. The dog wasn't such a huge fan of Mum and Dad kissing. I knew exactly how he felt.

Dad bent down and ruffled Oates's fur.

'I missed you too, big fella,' Dad said to him, and then he saw me eyeing the two bags of presents that were on the doorstep.

'Are those for me?' I asked.

'Some of them,' he said, with a wink. 'A lot of them, actually. Though I couldn't find any penguins. Wrong hemisphere. Some are for Mum, some for Ernest. There's even a squeaky toy reindeer for Oates.'

Oates barked.

'Now, Holly,' said Dad, 'I want you to tell me everything, starting from task one – don't leave anything out.'

* * *

The next morning, when I woke up, there was an envelope on the floor of my bedroom. I stared at it suspiciously, then got out of bed and picked it up. Dad's handwriting was on the front.

You didn't get a proper
birthday card this year. Sorry!
So here it is.
Better late than never, Holly!

I tore it open.

And the message inside:

To the best, most adventurous daughter that anyone's ever had. Love you times infinity – your very lucky dad.

✗

THE END

Dave Lowe grew up in Dudley in the West Midlands, and now lives in Brisbane, Australia, with his wife and two daughters. He spends his days writing books, drinking lots of tea, and treading on Lego that his daughters have left lying around. Dave's Stinky and Jinks books follow the adventures of a nine-year-old boy called Ben, and Stinky, Ben's genius pet hamster. (When Dave was younger, he had a pet hamster too. Unlike Stinky, however, Dave's hamster didn't often help him with his homework.) Find Dave online at @daveloweauthor or www.davelowebooks.com

Born in York in the late 1970s, **The Boy Fitz Hammond** now lives in Edinburgh with his wife and their two sons. A freelance illustrator for well over a decade, he loves to draw in a variety of styles, allowing him to work on a range of projects across all media. Find him online at www.nbillustration.co.uk/the-boy-fitz-hammond or on Twitter @tbfhDotCom

PRESS

Thank you for choosing a Piccadilly Press book.

If you would like to know more about our authors, our books or if you'd just like to know what we're up to, you can find us online.

www.piccadillypress.co.uk

You can also find us on:

We hope to see you soon!